Grace rea___ ___
placed it on her stomach.

It felt odd to touch her, especially since they'd spent the last five months making sure there was no physical contact between them. But there was contact now, and not just with Grace and him. Dutton also felt the slight thumps of the baby.

His breath went thin, and he got a surge of, well, he wasn't sure, but it felt good. For something so small, it certainly packed a punch, and in that moment, Dutton understood why parents gushed about their kids.

He looked at Grace and saw that she was smiling. He got that. She was able to feel these little miracle kicks even when things seemed so dangerous and uncertain.

His gaze automatically dropped to her mouth, and Dutton had to fight the overwhelming urge to kiss her.

HER BABY, HER BADGE

DELORES FOSSEN

INTRIGUE

**Harlequin®
INTRIGUE™**

Recycling programs
for this product may
not exist in your area.

ISBN-13: 978-1-335-45745-5

Her Baby, Her Badge

Copyright © 2025 by Delores Fossen

 Harlequin Enterprises ULC
22 Adelaide St. West, 41st Floor
Toronto, Ontario M5H 4E3, Canada
www.Harlequin.com

Printed in Lithuania

MIX
Paper | Supporting
responsible forestry
FSC® C021394

Delores Fossen, a *USA TODAY* bestselling author, has written over a hundred and fifty novels, with millions of copies of her books in print worldwide. She's received a Booksellers' Best Award and an RT Reviewers' Choice Best Book Award. She was also a finalist for a prestigious RITA® Award. You can contact the author through her website at www.deloresfossen.com.

Books by Delores Fossen

Harlequin Intrigue

Renegade Canyon

Her Baby, Her Badge

Saddle Ridge Justice

The Sheriff's Baby
Protecting the Newborn
Tracking Down the Lawman's Son

Child in Jeopardy

Silver Creek Lawman: Second Generation

Targeted in Silver Creek
Maverick Detective Dad
Last Seen in Silver Creek
Marked for Revenge

The Law in Lubbock County

Sheriff in the Saddle
Maverick Justice
Lawman to the Core
Spurred to Justice

Visit the Author Profile page at Harlequin.com.

CAST OF CHARACTERS

Sheriff Grace Granger—When she ends up on the hit list of a serial killer targeting female cops, she has to do whatever it takes to protect her unborn child. That includes teaming up with the baby's father, the very man Grace has spent years trying to resist.

Dutton McClennan—Even though the last thing he expected was to get Grace pregnant after a one-night stand, this former bad boy very much wants to be a father, and he won't let anyone hurt Grace or their baby.

Ike McClennan—Dutton's father despises any and all cops—and that includes Grace, the woman carrying his grandchild.

Wilson Finney—The county sheriff who has a grudge against Grace since she has the job he desperately wants. But would he kill her to get it?

Cassie Darnell—Dutton's ex, and she might want to get rid of Grace so she can try to reconcile with Dutton.

Brian Waterman—His fiancée's murder has been attributed to the serial killer who's targeting cops, but he could be responsible for her death.

Chapter One

The rain was washing away the blood.

That was Sheriff Grace Granger's second thought as she panned her flashlight over the scene. Her first thought had put ice in every vein in her body—the woman was dead.

Correction: the *cop* was dead.

The female officer was wearing a khaki-colored uniform, which meant she worked for the county sheriff and wasn't one of Grace's deputies in the Renegade Canyon Police Department. Still, that didn't lessen the overwhelming grief and the sickening feeling of dread that Grace felt.

"Get the tower lights set up here," Grace told her team of deputies, who'd responded to the 911 call with her. She pointed to two spots that were to the sides of the victim and far enough away from her that they wouldn't destroy any potential evidence.

The generator-powered lights were necessary to illuminate the scene so it could be examined. However, Grace needed no such illumination to see the dead woman. Her flashlight and the headlights of the responding vehicles were doing an effective job of that.

"Another one," Deputy Livvy Walsh muttered as she stepped shoulder-to-shoulder with Grace. She had no trouble hearing the slight tremble in her deputy's voice.

"Yes," Grace agreed. Her voice wasn't especially steady, either. Hard to be steady when taking in the scene in front of them.

The dead cop had been tied to a fence post in such a way that her head stayed upright, thanks to the thick rope around her neck. The killer had left her in her uniform, but he or she had shredded it so that parts of the fabric flapped in the stormy wind.

Although Grace didn't have any proof yet, the woman likely hadn't died on the post. Not if her manner of death was the same MO the killer had employed on another officer who'd been murdered a month earlier.

In that murder, San Antonio Detective Andrea Selby had been stabbed repeatedly, and then her killer had tied her to another fence post that was about a quarter of a mile from this particular one. And even though there was no evidence to link Detective Selby to Renegade Canyon, her body had been left just outside the grounds of the Mc-Clennan family's Towering Oaks Ranch. Which was in Grace's jurisdiction.

And she had personal ties to the ranch.

Very personal ties these days, she reminded herself as she thought of the baby bump that her high-visibility raincoat was concealing. Yes, her unborn child was about as personal as it got.

Unfortunately, every personal tie she had was also mixed with some bad blood that extended back to three generations of the McClennans and her own family. If there'd been only one murder, Grace might have been able to consider the location of the body a coincidence. But with two, this was a message. Exactly what message, Grace didn't know, but she needed to find out before another officer died.

"You okay?" Livvy asked her.

"No," Grace admitted. She blinked away the rain that was slapping at her. "And I figure you aren't, either." It was impossible to look at the cop's dead face and not see their own. Or future victims. "But we'll do our jobs."

Livvy made a sound of agreement that Grace knew wasn't merely lip service. They would indeed do their jobs and hopefully stop this killer from claiming anyone else.

"Any idea who she is?" Grace asked, tipping her head to the dead woman.

"No. She doesn't look familiar."

Grace was about to agree, but the slash of more headlights and the sounds of engines behind her had Grace looking over her shoulder. When she saw who'd arrived, she silently muttered a thanks.

And then a groan.

The thanks was for the CSI team who had just arrived, and they began to scramble from their van. Grace had contacted them immediately after she'd gotten the 911 call that there was a dead body, because she'd known this would be a race against the elements to preserve the scene. The spring storm was hitting hard and fast, and what the wind didn't destroy, the rain probably would.

Grace's groan was for the two men who exited a shiny silver truck with the Towering Oaks Ranch logo on the door. The family patriarch and all-around thorn in her side, Ike McClennan. And Dutton, his son. Except Dutton was more than just that. He was the reason for those "very personal ties" to his family ranch.

Since she didn't want any civilians trampling on the crime scene, Grace began to make her way to Ike and Dutton. With the glare of the headlights, it was hard for her to see Dutton's expression, but she figured he'd be concerned. One of his ranch hands had no doubt alerted him to the cop activity outside the fence, and not only would he want to know what was going on, but he would also want to make sure she was alright.

"What the hell happened?" Ike snarled. His rough voice thundered through the night.

He charged toward Grace, his gestures and sounds reminding her of a snorting bull. Ike might be approaching the seventy-year mark, but he still looked plenty strong and formidable with his six-foot, three-inch height and beefy build.

While Ike continued to move toward her, Grace stared him down. Or rather glared him down. She'd had plenty of practice doing it, and though this situation shouldn't be a confrontation, Ike usually managed to turn it into one any time she was involved.

"Well? What the hell is going on?" Ike persisted.

Dutton didn't move in front of his father and didn't do anything obvious to try to rein in the man. Grace hoped it stayed that way. Dutton, she knew, had a protective streak inside him. For their unborn baby. For Grace, too. But Grace didn't want him acting on that. Tonight, she was the badge, and not his ex-lover and the mother of his child.

"You can't be here," Grace told Ike. "This is a crime scene."

Of course, that didn't set well with Ike, who looked ready to implode, so Grace just hiked her thumb in the direction of the fence post. And the body.

That stopped Ike in his tracks, and when his attention landed on the dead woman, he cursed. "Another one," he said on a groan.

Dutton cursed, too, but his profanity stayed under his breath. He looked at her, combing his intense brown eyes over her face, no doubt checking for any signs of injury.

Or stress. The stress would be there. Nothing she could do about that. But there wasn't a mark on her.

"I didn't find the body," she told him. "An anonymous call came in through Dispatch. The caller said we'd find the body tied to a fence post outside the west side of the ranch."

And since a nearly identical call had come in with the first murder a month earlier, that's how Grace had known it was almost certainly the real deal. Still, she had hoped for the best. Obviously, though, the best hadn't happened.

"You haven't done a good job of stopping this, have you?" Ike muttered, shaking his head in disgust.

"No, I haven't," Grace admitted, and that sickened her.

It didn't matter that the killer hadn't left any traceable forensic evidence and there'd been no witnesses to either the murder or the body dump. It was her job to keep the community safe, and she was failing at that, big-time.

She shoved aside the pity party that threatened, but this felt like a serious jab at her professionalism, while her private life had had its own jabs. Including the "jab" standing in front of her.

Dutton.

He was still staring at her with those intense eyes. Ironic, since the rest of Dutton was the opposite of intense. Everything else about him was normally laid-back. The easy stride of his lanky body. That quick smile that only made his face even hotter than usual. The smooth drawl that she was certain had worked in his favor too many times to count.

"No wonder you can't solve this," Ike went on. "You need better hired help."

The venom in his voice went up a notch, and Grace didn't have to guess why. She followed his narrowed gaze to his other son, Deputy Rory McClennan, who had just finished setting up one of the lights. Grace wasn't the only one who had to deal with bad blood with Ike. Rory did as well, by basically turning his back on his dad and becoming a cop.

"Mr. McClennan," Grace said, "as I've already informed you, this is a crime scene, and you should just go home."

Of course, that earned her a huff from the man, but he finally moved away from her and back toward the truck. What he didn't do was get in. Despite the storm taking swipes at him, he leaned against the hood and stared out at the responders and cops.

Dutton didn't leave, either. Nor did he go to the truck, as his father had done. He stayed right by Grace's side, and Livvy must've decided to give them a moment, because she stepped away.

"This is the same as the other one," Dutton said. Not a question, and he could certainly see the similarities for himself. "What kind of precautions are you going to take?" he asked. "And I know I'm making you plenty mad just by asking that, but I'd like to know."

She sighed. "I'll be as careful as I can be. But I'll also do my job," she said, certain that he'd known that was how she would respond.

Dutton didn't say anything about that not being enough. And that had to be hard for him. Because he was just as invested in this baby as she was.

"If I can help, let me," he muttered.

Not a pushy demand. Again, that had to be difficult for him since Dutton was a man used to being in charge. Not a growling-bear kind of in charge like his father, but the real deal. These days, Ike was just a figurehead on the ranch. Dutton owned it and ran it his way despite what seemed to be constant criticism and interference from Ike.

Grace made eye contact with him. A mistake. Whenever she was this close to Dutton, she was flooded with memories. And not all were bad, just unwanted. Of course, the heat she felt for him was unwanted, too, but she just couldn't seem to make it go away.

That heat had made life a whole lot more difficult for both of them, and sometimes it felt as if the two of them were caught up in a feud, like the Hatfields and McCoys. Or rather, they would have been caught up if they hadn't decided years ago to keep their distance from each other. And that had worked.

Until five months ago.

That's when things had gone south after what had essentially been a shootout at the ranch between the McClennans and thieves who'd tried to steal some champion horses. Grace and several of her deputies had been involved in the gunfight. Dutton, too. And after surviving a near-death experience, the adrenaline and heat had landed a double punch that had in turn landed them in bed.

Grace hadn't looked up the stats of getting pregnant from what was essentially a one-night stand, but it had happened. And now here she was. Both she and her baby caught in the cross fire between the McClennans and pretty much everyone else in Renegade Canyon.

Dutton glanced over his shoulder and muttered some profanity under his breath. At first, she thought his father was heading back their way, but Ike was still by the truck. Still glaring. A new visitor had arrived in a county cruiser and had parked next to the McClennan truck.

County Sheriff Wilson Finney.

Grace knew the man better than she wanted to. Dutton likely could say the same. Wilson had been born and raised in Renegade Canyon, but when he'd lost the sheriff's election to Grace six years earlier, he'd moved and had eventually become the county sheriff.

Wilson donned a raincoat over his toned and heavily muscled body and made his way toward her. Or rather, toward the dead cop. He stopped right outside the crime-scene tape that the CSIs had already set up, and stared at the woman who'd once been his deputy. Wilson cursed, too, and it wasn't under his breath. He stood there several more moments before he turned toward Grace.

And scowled.

Grace wasn't sure if the facial expression was for her or Dutton. Maybe both. But Wilson didn't even attempt to rein it in.

"Sleeping with the enemy," Wilson growled. His gaze dropped to her stomach, and even though he couldn't see her baby bump under her raincoat, he knew it was there. Grace suspected everyone in the county did. "Why haven't you arrested him yet?" he demanded.

By *him*, Grace had no doubts whom he meant. "Dutton doesn't have a criminal record."

"Only because he hasn't been caught." Wilson stopped directly in front of them and propped his hands on his hips. The glare was still firmly in place. "That whole family should be locked up, and you should be fired for sleeping with him."

Even though Dutton wasn't touching her, Grace could practically feel every muscle in his body tense. Not because of the insult to him. But because of the insult to her.

Grace decided to try to nip this in the bud. "Sheriff Finney," she said, purposely addressing him by his title and surname to remind him this was work and not some free-for-all at a bar, "since you're probably in shock and grieving for your fallen deputy, I'll give you some leeway on that. *Some*," Grace emphasized.

"I won't," Dutton snarled, and there was a lethal edge to his voice. An apparently effective one.

Wilson stared at him and must have decided this was not a fight he needed to launch into tonight, because the county sheriff shook his head, cursed and then pinned his attention back on the murdered deputy. Grace gave Wilson a few more moments before she said anything.

"Tell me about her," Grace began.

Judging from the long pause, Wilson wanted to hang on to his temper a bit longer, but he finally spoke. "Deputy Elaine Sneed. She's been on the job for less than a year."

Grace waited, expecting more, but more didn't come. She sighed and took out her phone. Now that she had a name, she tapped into the database to retrieve what info she could.

"Sneed," Dutton repeated. "Is she Frank Sneed's daughter?"

"You know her?" Grace asked, and as the deputy's bio loaded, she could confirm that Elaine was indeed the daughter of Frank and Marion Sneed from Carson, a town about twenty miles away.

"Frank recently bought some horses from me," Dutton explained. "And he brought his daughter with him to pick them up." He, too, had another look at the dead woman. "That looks like her."

"It is," Grace confirmed, since Elaine was the Sneeds' only child. "She was twenty-four and had been a county deputy for eighteen months." So slightly longer than Wilson had guessed. Strange that he wouldn't have known that about one of his people, but then, maybe he wasn't a hands-on boss.

"She was young. I didn't give her any of the hard cases,"

Wilson volunteered, but Grace had the feeling he just wanted to contribute something that wouldn't make him seem so clueless when it came to someone who'd worked for him for a year and a half.

"She's engaged," Dutton informed them. "Or maybe already married. Frank mentioned that."

"She's not married," Grace said, referring to the bio. "Or if she is, she didn't update it in her records." She paused, looked at Wilson. "I need to be at the death notification of her next of kin, but I'm assuming you'll want to be the one to deliver the actual news?"

"Why do you need to be there?" Wilson snapped. "She worked for me."

"And she was killed, or at least her body was left in my jurisdiction," Grace quickly pointed out. "This is my investigation, and you know the protocol. I need to talk to her next of kin."

Sadly, that was because the killer was often someone close to the victim. Grace didn't think that was the situation here, but she had to go by the book.

Wilson looked ready to argue with her, but the head CSI, Larry Crandall, called out before Wilson could launch into anything.

"Sheriff Granger," Larry said. "There's a note on the body."

That got Grace's attention, but she didn't charge forward to take a look. She had to hold out her arm, though, to stop Wilson from doing just that.

Grace moved her flashlight over the body and saw the edge of a plastic bag that was tucked in the deputy's shirt. The CSI eased it out, then held it up for Grace to see. Yes, it was a note alright. A handwritten one. And whoever had put it there had no doubt encased it in that bag to make sure it didn't get soaked.

"What does it say?" Grace asked, since she wasn't able to make out the words from where she was standing.

The CSI turned it toward him, and started to scan it, then muttered something she didn't catch before he read it aloud.

"'Two down. Sheriff Grace Granger, you're on the list, too, and your time is coming. Or should I say ending? And for you, I'll add a bonus. Two for the price of one. You and Dutton McClennan. Soon, you'll both be dead.'"

Chapter Two

While Dutton waited in Grace's office, he paced and continued to read through reports from his ranch hands and his PI that were coming in on his phone. Something he'd been doing for the past two hours as he waited for Grace to return from notifying Deputy Elaine Sneed's family that she was dead.

Dutton knew he wouldn't be included in that tough job, but he wished he'd been allowed to go, anyway. And not just so he would have been close to Grace to make sure she was safe. That was a huge concern. However, he also needed answers as to why Grace and he were now targets of a killer.

Well, maybe they were.

Thanks to a copy of the threatening note now pinned to Grace's board in her office, Dutton could see the words, the threat, every time he paced in front of it. Which was often. Even though Grace was the sheriff and therefore the top cop, her office wasn't huge by anyone's standards. More of a bare-bones kind of place, designed for work and not much else.

He suspected that over the fifty or so years that the office of the Renegade Canyon PD had been here at this particular location, there'd been plenty of work done in this space. At the very desk that had once been occupied by

Grace's mother, Aileen, and before that, Grace's grand-father, Chet. Before that, there'd been cousins at the helm at the original police station. A string of Granger sheriffs going back over a century.

A law-enforcement legacy that Grace had continued.

Normally, thinking of her as the sheriff didn't put a knot in Dutton's gut. It was simply who she was and had been for six years.

Of course, *simply* hadn't always been, well, simple.

Not with his own family legacy that was often at odds with Grace and her family. Still, he had always thought Grace as capable of balancing that feud, this forbidden at-traction they had for each other and anything to do with the badge.

But that note changed things.

Two down. Sheriff Grace Granger, you're on the list, too, and your time is coming. Or should I say ending? And for you, I'll add a bonus. Two for the price of one. You and Dutton McClennan. Soon, you'll both be dead.

Yeah, no way could Dutton be unaffected by that. Grace and he might not be an actual couple, but in four months or so, they'd become parents. And if Grace's life was in danger, then so was the baby's. That more than tightened his gut. It twisted at everything inside him.

It twisted even more when he had to mentally spell out something he already knew. That Grace wouldn't want him to play protector in this. In fact, she'd want to protect *him*. Not because of their past, but because he was now the job to her.

Dutton would need to figure out a way around that. He wanted Grace focusing on her own safety. On the baby's. And that would involve shoving aside their past so they could work together.

Which wouldn't be easy.

Especially since the past was front and center between them. Not only the baby, but also the scalding attraction they'd fought for years. A fight they'd lost just twice. Once when they'd been teenagers and had become each other's "firsts." Then again, five months ago, when she'd gotten pregnant. It was easier to fight the attraction when they weren't around each other, but that note would make any distancing impossible.

But they needed some emotional barriers.

Their families would make it next to impossible for them to be together and still live and work in this small town. The bickering and conflicts would escalate, and Ike would make Grace's life as miserable as possible.

Dutton glanced at the movement in the doorway. Not Grace or one of the deputies, who had likely been instructed to babysit him and make sure he didn't go anywhere. This was a black cat that strolled in as if he owned the place. With only the arrogance that a cat and a Greek god could have managed, the cat eyed Dutton and then sauntered past him to leap into Grace's chair.

He knew the cat's name was Sherlock. Knew, too, that the police department had more or less adopted him after he'd been found standing guard over his late owner's body.

Not a murder but a heart attack.

The plan had been for Grace to take Sherlock to the county animal shelter, but since that'd been four months ago, Dutton figured the feline was here to stay. Especially since he'd noticed that someone had added an automated litter box and feeding area in the break room.

Dutton stopped pacing at the sound of approaching footsteps, and turned to see his brother, Deputy Rory McClennan, step into the doorway. Genetically, they looked like twins, with their black hair, dark brown eyes and nearly identical McClennan DNA, but Rory was five years younger than Dutton and therefore the baby of the family.

Rory handed Dutton a cup of coffee and sipped his own while his cop's eyes studied his big brother. He didn't ask Dutton if he was okay. No need. He wasn't. He was shaken to the core, and while that wouldn't have been obvious to most people, Rory would have seen it.

"Grace is on her way back," Rory said. "She'll be here in a couple of minutes."

"Any idea how the notification went?" Dutton asked.

Rory shrugged, which was apparently all the info he was going to dole out. They were brothers, but Dutton knew that Rory was a solid cop, one who was loyal to his boss, and he would want any info about the notification to come not from him, but from Grace herself.

Rory tipped his head to Dutton's phone and then the note on the board. "How exactly are you looking into that?" his brother asked.

"The same way I've been looking into it for the past month." Since the first body had been left just outside the ranch.

Even though there'd been no threatening note left on that victim, Dutton had had to consider that the location of the body hadn't been random. That the death of San Antonio Detective Andrea Selby was somehow linked to his family, and the ranch.

Or to him specifically.

After all, Towering Oaks might be considered the McClennan family ranch, but Dutton was the owner and had been since he'd turned twenty-one.

Despite the tensions it had created with his dad, his mother had transferred ownership to Dutton as a birthday gift. It had been a nasty little twist in their family littered with nasty twists, and Ike hadn't been able to stop it because Dutton's mom had never given any portion of the ranch to Ike when he'd moved there after they'd married.

The Towering Oaks had belonged to Dutton's mom's parents, and when they'd passed, they had made her the sole owner of the place, an ownership that his mom hadn't tried to change to include her husband. That, and many other things in their marriage, had created a rift that still existed when his mother had died six months ago.

Dutton hadn't found any connections to the first murder victim, and he'd looked. Hard. So had Grace and all of her deputies, including Rory. After all, his father had made plenty of enemies over the years. Dutton had, too. Ditto for Grace and her own family of cops. But so far, there wasn't anything to link Detective Selby to Grace or them.

Now this new murder had to be factored into what they already knew. And judging from the note, the two dead cops were indeed connected in some way. In exactly what way, Dutton didn't know, but he'd instructed the PI, Jake Winters, whom he kept on retainer to dig deep into Elaine Sneed's life, and look for any association she might have had with the first murdered woman.

The PI had gotten right on the assignment and for the past two hours had been sending Dutton info he was gathering. So far, Dutton didn't see anything in those updates that gave him the answers he needed.

Rory stepped out of the doorway moments after Dutton heard the approaching footsteps. He felt his body automatically rev up. Cursed his reaction and saw the same mental cursing on Grace's face when she came into her office. Even though their gazes only held for a couple of seconds, the usual intensity was there.

And the blasted heat.

Of course, there was something else in the mix now. That razor-sharp concern for each other and their child.

"The parents aren't suspects," Grace said right off the bat. "Airtight alibis and no motive. Learning about Elaine's death crushed them," she added in a murmur.

Dutton hadn't thought for one minute that the parents had murdered their daughter, but it was good to have them ruled out. Especially since their suspect pool included anyone who had a beef with Grace, him or the two dead cops.

"Did County Sheriff Finney come back with you?" Rory asked.

"No," she answered.

A muscle flickered in Grace's jaw, and Dutton suspected Wilson Finney had continued to act like the jerk that he could be when it came to Grace. Everyone knew the jerk behavior was because Grace had beaten him in the election for the town sheriff, and because of it, Grace and Wilson usually gave each other a wide berth. Just as she and Dutton did. But again, that couldn't happen in this investigation.

"You and I need to talk," she said to Dutton.

It wasn't his imagination that she sounded all cop. She clearly wanted to draw some lines here. Those lines, for the time being, were that she wasn't viewing him as her baby's father, but as the target of a killer. Her goal would no doubt be to do what she could to ensure his safety and then get him out of her office.

Dutton was going to have something to say about that, though.

Grace peeled off her rain gear, hanging it on the wall pegs. Despite the gear, the storm had gotten to her, and her dark blond hair was wet and pressed to her head and neck.

She wasn't pale, not exactly, but Dutton could see the un-steadiness on her face and in her cool green eyes.

Eyes that she pinned to the board.

She studied it. The note that'd been added. Elaine's photo, too. Not one from the crime scene. This was a pic-ture taken from the county sheriff's webpage, where the fresh-faced deputy was in uniform and trying to look stern. She hadn't quite accomplished that, in Dutton's opinion.

There was another photo pinned to the other side of the board. This one was of the first murdered cop, San Antonio Detective Andrea Selby. Beneath the pictures, the names of about two dozen suspects had been written in.

And all crossed off except for two.

Dutton was familiar with both of them. They were men whom Detective Selby had arrested, and they had recently been released from prison. Even though they were still on the board, it was because they didn't have alibis and not because there was any evidence to link them to her death.

Now Grace and the deputies would need to add suspect names beneath Elaine's photo. Dutton had already started the process. Not on a board, but mentally, with the info his PI was gathering for him.

"I'll see if I can get an update from the CSIs," Rory said, no doubt heading back to his desk in the bullpen.

Dutton figured his brother would indeed check for up-dates, but Rory was also likely giving him some time alone with Grace. Time she wouldn't want, but Dutton needed it.

"So why leave us a note?" Dutton asked. "Did the killer warn or threaten the SAPD detective before she was mur-dered?"

When Sherlock bounded out of the chair and went to rub against her legs, Grace shook her head and bent down to scratch the cat's head. "Nothing has come up about that, and considering how visible the killer made this note, I think if there had been some kind of premurder threat, then we would have found it."

That was what Dutton figured. "So this is meant to scare us," he concluded. "To make us keep watch over our shoulders and lose sleep."

Which it would do. But Dutton had no intention of running scared. No. He had every intention of finding this snake and making him pay for the hell this was causing the families of the victims, Grace and everyone else involved.

"Sheriff Finney suggested you and I were the reason his deputy was murdered," Grace said, standing upright again, and he could tell from her tone that the suggestion had hit her hard.

Because there could possibly be some truth to it.

Neither Grace nor he had done anything intentional to provoke these deaths, and they certainly weren't to blame. But the guilt was there, rolling right through them. Someone might be killing female cops to get back at them for something. Then again, maybe it was to get back at someone else and the two of them were simply targets on a killer's list.

"How much did *Sheriff* Wilson Finney hassle you tonight?" Dutton asked, and he added some venom to the man's title. Venom that Wilson aimed at them every chance he got.

Grace dragged in a long breath. "He thinks I should be fired." She slid her hand over her baby bump. "Then again, so do a lot of people."

Dutton sighed and did some silent cursing. What he didn't do was touch her even though that's what he wanted to do. He wanted to try to ease some of that tension he saw on her face, but touching her would do the opposite of that.

He couldn't argue with Grace about a lot of people wanting her fired. Plenty of people in town hated him and his family, which meant they hated Grace being pregnant with his child.

Thankfully, though, there were enough members of the town council who were staving off a recall election that would oust Grace. Maybe because those members thought the pregnancy had nothing to do with the excellent job Grace had done. Maybe, too, Grace's mother, Aileen, still had enough influence to keep her daughter where she was. That despite Aileen not approving of Dutton, his family or the pregnancy.

Since there was no way either of them wanted to dwell on the opinions of the town or the county sheriff, Dutton moved on to something she needed to know. "After the first murder, I had more security cameras installed."

Grace's head whipped up. "I didn't see any cameras."

"Long-range ones with night vision that are motion-activated. They're mounted on trees along the fence line. But before you get your hopes up, the angles of the cameras in that area might not be right to capture who did this. Or the person might not have gotten in range to trigger the motion activation. The security company is downloading any feed now and will send it to both of us as soon as they have it."

Though he'd said that part about not getting her hopes up, the news seemed to do just that. Some of the tension in her face eased just a little. Capturing the killer on camera was a long shot, but it was better than what they had now—which was pretty much nothing.

Dutton's phone dinged with a text. "From my PI," he muttered, reading through the latest bit of info. "According to what he told his boss, Elaine's fiancé has been in El Paso on business for the past three days. He's a real-estate agent, and he went there to meet with some bigwig client. FYI, he works for Elaine's parents. They own the real-estate agency."

Grace didn't ask if that alibi was confirmed. She'd want to do that herself, but she went to the board and wrote "Brian Waterman, fiancé, person of interest." Since Dutton hadn't told her the man's name, she had obviously already run her own background check.

"I spoke to Brian Waterman on the phone on the drive back here," she volunteered. "If he killed Elaine, then he did a top-notch job of covering up his guilt. He sounded just as broken as her parents. *Sounded*. But he stays on the list until we can confirm his alibi." She paused a heartbeat. "Tell me who you believe killed her and who's coming after us."

"I don't know," he admitted, and that brought on more silent cursing. "I'm having my PI look for broader connections. Those with possible grudges against female cops. Those with grudges against us." Dutton handed her his phone, and he felt the trickle of heat when his fingers brushed against hers.

Yeah, this was why touching her was a bad idea.

"So far, this is what the PI has come up with," Dutton explained.

It was a list, a very long one, of known criminals in the state who'd made public threats against cops—specifically female ones. Threats either posted on social media or actually made during arrests and court proceedings.

"Dozens," she said on a sigh.

There were indeed dozens, and Dutton suspected other names would be added to the list as the PI continued to dig. Grace and her deputies would no doubt tack on even more potentials. Which meant there had to be a way to narrow it down.

"You'll be stretching your resources thin if you try to investigate every single one of them," Dutton pointed out. "My PI can help, though, if you're willing to let a civilian in on this."

If Grace heard his offer, she didn't respond. Something had obviously grabbed her attention.

"Avery Kenney," she said, and she hurried behind her desk to boot up her laptop. "His name came up in the first investigation…"

Her voice trailed off while her gaze flew over the screen. Dutton had figured that many of the names on his PI's list had also been on Grace's, and he went to stand next to her so he could see the info she was accessing.

"Yes, Avery Kenney, a bartender from San Antonio." She highlighted the name. "He was shot by a female officer who mistook him for a burglar. Lots of angry posts on social media about how the officer should have never been given a badge since she was overly emotional and clearly 'not ready for duty.'" She put that last part in quotes.

"You interviewed him?" Dutton asked.

She scrolled farther down the screen. "Yes. But it was a phone interview since Kenney was out of state at the time. His boss vouched for his alibi, but I got a bad feeling about him. Enough so that I drove to San Antonio to see him. He said in a not-so-friendly way that he'd already answered my questions and that if I wanted to talk to him again, I'd have to go through his lawyer."

"I'm guessing since he had already given you those answers, you didn't have enough to force him to come in for further questioning?" Dutton asked.

Grace nodded and she tapped the two former prisoners' names beneath Detective Selby's photo. Charlie Salvetti and Teddy Gonzales. "Because of their criminal records,

I did bring them in." She sighed, shook her head. "And I got absolutely no hint of guilt. Maybe they're just good at hiding it."

She didn't sound convinced of that last possibility. Neither was Dutton. He hadn't interviewed the pair, but he'd had his PI research them. Dutton had ruled out Salvetti because he was five feet, two inches tall and weighed 120 pounds. He likely wouldn't have been able to lift the dead women and stage them against the fence posts. The second man, Teddy Gonzales, was nearly seventy, and while he had the size, Dutton didn't think he had the strength. Added to that, there was no proof that either man was familiar with Renegade Canyon or the ranch.

Dutton's phone dinged again just as Grace got the signal for an incoming email. "It's the video from the security cameras," he pointed out, and he stayed right by Grace's side while she downloaded it to her computer.

The dark footage appeared on her screen. Emphasis on *dark*. And the rain certainly didn't help. It was like looking through a gray gauzy curtain. But the fact there was footage meant something or someone had activated it, and Dutton was hoping that was a good sign they'd managed to film the killer.

Grace scrolled through the first part of the feed, zooming in on what had triggered the motion-activation feature. A deer with its eyes casting an eerie glow in the night. Dutton checked to see the location of this specific camera, and he guessed it was a good thousand yards from the part of the fence where the body had been left.

She moved on to the next camera feed. And zoomed in when there was some motion. Not a deer this time. This was a person. Specifically, a person dragging something.

The killer with the body.

Grace made a soft sound, a moan that she obviously had tried to silence, but Dutton heard it. Felt it, too, since he was experiencing that same sense of dread that Grace no doubt was.

She slowed the footage, continuing to zoom in as much as she could. The killer was wearing what appeared to be a long dark raincoat with a large hood that completely concealed his or her head and face. It reminded Dutton of the images of the grim reaper, and it was grim alright, since the camera had managed to capture the dead body.

It was definitely Deputy Elaine Sneed.

"Move so I can see your face," Grace muttered, obviously speaking to the killer.

But the person didn't cooperate and kept his or her head angled down. It was also possible the person was wearing a balaclava, which had created a black-hole effect.

"Based on the size, I can't tell if it's a man or woman," Grace added.

"Neither can I, and the fact the killer is dragging rather than carrying means it doesn't have to be a big person." He mentally shrugged. "Still, dragging takes some strength, especially since this point is about hundred yards or so from the road."

This time the sound Grace made was one of agreement, and they continued to watch as the killer stopped by the fence post and hoisted up the body. And it was indeed a body and not an unconscious deputy. There was already blood all over the uniform.

Dutton tried to keep his breathing level as they saw the killer coil the rope around the dead cop. Despite the rain, it took less than a minute to secure it in place before the killer stepped back as if to admire the work.

And then, the murderer looked up.

Directly at the camera.

Hell. That gave Dutton a jolt, and he'd been right about the balaclava, or maybe it was a mask, because the only part of the face that was visible was the strip that exposed the eyes. Definitely not enough to make any kind of identification.

While still looking up at the camera, the killer reached into the raincoat pocket and extracted something. Exactly what, Dutton couldn't tell, because it was wrapped in what appeared to be black cloth. The person used it to point at the camera in a threatening gesture that seemed to say "you're next" and then flung it over the fence and onto the ranch.

Grace whipped out her phone, and Dutton didn't have to guess whom she was calling. The CSIs.

"Check over the fence now, in the area behind the fence post," she said to the person who answered. "The killer left something for us."

Chapter Three

Grace stared at her phone, willing it to ring so the CSIs could tell her what they'd found. She had thought it would only take them a couple of minutes.

Apparently not, since it was going on a half hour now.

She had used the time to continue viewing the security-camera footage to make sure the killer hadn't returned to the scene to retrieve whatever had been tossed. But she didn't see anything. In fact, there were no signs of anyone other than what Dutton and she had already viewed. So they'd watched and rewatched frame by frame as the killer had dragged and posed the body.

The crime lab would view the footage, too, and Grace was hoping they'd see something that the two of them had missed. While she was hoping, she added that maybe there'd be some usable forensic evidence left on the body. Or in the bag that'd been tossed onto the ranch. Because right now, she essentially had nothing that could help her prevent another murder.

Including Dutton's. And her own.

Yes, that was weighing heavily on her mind, and she was certain it was the same for Dutton. After all, these were the highest stakes, since their precious baby could be at risk.

"The killer seemed to know the location of the security camera," Grace pointed out.

Dutton's quick agreement let her know he'd already considered that, and he took out his phone. "I'm forwarding you the contact info of the security company I used in case an employee there is the killer. Not likely since the employees are heavily vetted." He fired off the text to her and started another one. "I'm also sending you a list of all my ranch hands. Again, they're heavily vetted."

She doubted they'd find the killer's name on the lists, but again, she'd check. "How many people knew you had the cameras installed?" she asked.

"Plenty," he admitted. "The security company had a big truck with their logo, and the installers would have parked in that part of the pasture. So basically, anyone driving by could have seen it."

True, and gossip about the cameras would have gotten around. It hadn't gotten back to Grace, but then people usually shied away from talking to her about Dutton.

"Are the cameras visible from the road during the day?" she asked.

His forehead bunched up while he gave that question some thought. "Probably. The idea wasn't to conceal them. It was to record the killer if there was a return visit."

Which there obviously had been. And maybe the killer had worn that bulky raincoat because of the storm, but it had served double duty of concealing the killer's body and face.

"There has to be a reason the killer threw that bag onto the ranch," Dutton said a moment later. "Maybe to extend the crime scene? To put you in the position of having to deal with my dad and question us about it?"

Grace had already gone there and had to agree it was a

possibility. A way of adding one more thing to an already complex situation. And part of that complexity was she would indeed have to investigate Dutton and his family. Heck, she already had after the first murder.

"Still," Dutton went on, "the bodies were practically on the ranch grounds, anyway."

"Yes," she agreed. "But there's a subtle difference between practically and actually on it. This is an escalation of sorts."

She tapped a name that had been crossed off on the board. The name of the person who actually owned the land where the bodies had been dragged and staged. Elmer Dawson. He was in his nineties and in assisted living. Grace suspected that once Elmer passed away, his next of kin would be selling the acres, and Dutton would buy them.

"I couldn't find a single connection between Elmer Dawson and the first murdered woman," Grace revealed. "And I suspect there won't be one between him and the second woman, either. Still, I'll check," she added on a heavy sigh.

Before she could add more to that, her phone rang. "It's the CSIs," she announced and immediately answered it. She didn't put the call on speaker, but she figured Dutton was standing close enough to her that he could hear Larry Crandall's voice.

"We got the bag," Larry said. "It took us a while to find it because the rain had caused some mud and grass to cover it." He paused. "It's a knife, and there's some blood on the blade and in the bag itself."

Grace drew in a sharp breath. "The murder weapon."

"Possibly," Larry admitted. "We've got it bagged, but I'll take a picture of it and send it to you. It's not an ordinary knife. It's got some fancy carvings on the handle."

Maybe that meant it'd be easier to trace. But if so, Grace

had to wonder why the killer would have left it behind. This could be part of the cat-and-mouse game that the killer seemed to be playing.

"I'll send you a picture in a couple of minutes," Larry added, then ended the call.

Grace didn't even have time to put her phone in her pocket before someone stepped into her office doorway, and it wasn't one of her deputies. However, it was a familiar face.

Cassie Darnell.

Not exactly a welcome visitor. Along with owning several businesses, including the town's only fitness center, she was also on the town council. The very council that had considered trying to oust Grace when word had gotten around that she was pregnant with Dutton's baby. But Cassie was more than that.

The woman was also Dutton's ex-girlfriend.

Even though Dutton and Cassie had broken up nearly a year ago, months before Grace had gotten pregnant, it was still awkward for Grace to be around her. It was probably the same for Dutton, too, since Grace had heard the breakup hadn't been Cassie's idea.

Cassie had already opened her mouth to say something, but she froze in the doorway with her gaze fixed on Dutton and Grace. And Cassie had no doubt noticed that the two of them were standing close, arm to arm. Grace refrained from stepping away from him. It would only make them look even more guilty of some PDA at the police station.

"Oh," Cassie said, her voice filled with the surprise already on her face.

A classically beautiful face, Grace noted, to go along with her golden blond hair and blue eyes. A striking set of features that explained why Dutton had likely been attracted to the woman in the first place. That and Cassie's perfectly toned, athletic body. Cassie looked as if she could have been a model for the posters hanging in the fitness center.

"Dutton," Cassie began, "I didn't know you'd be here."

Now Grace did move, but it was to cover the board. Cassie might be on the town council, but that didn't make her privy to the details of an investigation. The same could be said for Dutton even though he did have more than a personal interest in this case.

"I'm giving the sheriff some info," Dutton replied.

It wasn't a lie. He had indeed given her those lists, and Grace welcomed picking his brain for possibilities as to the identity of the killer.

But it wasn't the full truth, either.

Grace knew he was there because he was worried about the baby and her.

"Good," Cassie said. "I hope you catch the killer soon." She paused. "That's why I'm here. I got a call from Wilson."

Grace held back a groan. Dutton didn't. "Was he whining to you about how Grace is handling the investigation?" Dutton asked.

Cassie nodded, and her face flushed a little. "He asked me to press the rest of the town council not only to oust Grace from the case, but also to push for the recall vote to try to get rid of her as sheriff. I reminded him that the town council doesn't get involved in the day-to-day dealings of police business, but Wilson insisted this was a conflict of interest for you. He feels he should take over since it was his deputy who was murdered."

"If you use that logic, then the lieutenant at SAPD should take over since his detective was the first death," Grace quickly pointed out. She tried to keep any anger out of her tone. Hard to do, though. "Both bodies were in my juris-diction. I'm staying on the case." Grace didn't bother to address the part about Wilson pressing her to be ousted.

Cassie nodded again. "I figured you'd say that. But I thought you should know he insisted he'd be calling other members of the council. And the Texas Rangers."

"The Rangers?" Dutton asked.

"Wilson thinks Grace is out of her depth and that she should have already asked them for assistance."

"I'm considering it," Grace admitted. "But until two hours ago, it was a single murder that might or might not be connected to Dutton, me or the town. Once the current crime scene has been processed, I'll consider whether or not to bring in the Rangers."

The Texas Rangers were similar to the FBI, but on a state level. The Rangers only assisted when requested. Now that she had two bodies and the threatening note, Grace almost certainly would ask for support in processing the evidence. The Ranger crime lab could likely do that much faster than the county one.

"I hate to say this," Cassie went on, "but Wilson sounded...enraged. He really despises you, Grace. You, too, Dutton. He still blames you for firing his father as ranch foreman."

"I fired him because I caught him stealing supplies," Dutton reminded her.

That'd been years ago, when Grace had been a deputy, and Wilson was indeed still sporting a grudge about that. Wilson felt as if that'd played into him not winning the elec-tion. Played into his father's death, too, since he'd died a broken man about six months ago. His cause of death was a heart attack, but Wilson insisted it'd been brought on by stress caused by Dutton.

"I think Wilson's going to push and push to make things harder for you," Cassie said, aiming that comment at Grace.

Great. Just what she didn't need, with a double-homicide investigation and with the town council breathing down her neck. Every move and decision she made would be scrutinized to the hilt. Then again, that had been happening, anyway.

Cassie checked her watch and then glanced out the window at the rain that was continuing to pelt against the glass. "Well, I should be getting home."

"Late night for you," Grace commented.

Cassie attempted a smile that didn't quite succeed. "I was catching up on some paperwork. That's where I was when Wilson called me."

Grace didn't ask why Cassie had decided to deliver the news of that call tonight, when it was already going on midnight, but she didn't miss the longing glance Cassie gave Dutton. Yes, longing. Apparently, the woman still had feelings for him and wasn't doing a good job of hiding it.

"Good night," Cassie added and headed out.

Dutton waited until Cassie was out of earshot before he whispered, "Could Wilson have murdered those two cops?" he asked. "Cassie was right about him despising both of us."

"He does indeed," Grace agreed. She shook her head, though. "But it'd be beyond extreme for him to kill just to make our lives miserable."

The moment she said the words, Grace realized there could be more to it than that. Wilson wanted her job, period. And he wanted to get back at Dutton for firing his father. So if Wilson had gone off the deep end—and that was a massive *if*—he could be masterminding these murders to make Grace look bad while also dragging Dutton into the investigation.

"I think you should at least consider Wilson a possible suspect," Dutton commented.

Oh, she would. Grace just wouldn't put his name on the board, but she intended to look into the possibility that she was dealing with a dirty cop. Of course, that was just one thing she had to deal with. Another was standing right next to her.

She turned toward the board and tapped the note the killer had left. Specifically, she pointed to his name. "Because of that, I should put you in protective custody. *Should*," Grace stressed.

"My house on the ranch is more secure than any place you could arrange for me," Dutton quickly pointed out. "In fact, it'd be safer for you and the baby to be there, too."

"Probably," she admitted. "But there's no way I'm staying at your ranch."

"You wouldn't be staying with my family," he insisted. "You'd be staying in a guestroom at my house on the ranch."

She was well aware of that and knew that Ike lived in the main house, even though it, too, belonged to Dutton. Dutton had basically given it to him after he'd had his own place built when he'd been in his early twenties.

Ike didn't live alone in the massive mansion, though, but resided with his much younger brother, Asher, and his wife, Kitty. They had an adopted twelve-year-old daughter, Jamie, who, because of the big age difference, was more of a niece to Dutton than a cousin.

"It's still *your* house, on *your* ranch," Grace pointed out.

Dutton opened his mouth, probably to launch into a lecture about her not letting the gossip play into where she stayed, but he closed his mouth just as fast. He knew what a complicated situation this was for both of them.

"So you'll go back to your place, turn on any and all

security systems you have and shut your gate to visitors," she stated.

He gave her a flat look. "Will you do all those things at your place? Wait," he continued. "You don't have a gate to keep out killers, and you live out in the middle of nowhere with no neighbor in sight."

That was true. No gate. She lived on what had once been her grandparents' horse ranch, and her nearest neighbor was over a half mile away. Normally, that suited her just fine, but this was the first time she had a killer targeting her. Still, she wasn't going to let this SOB run her out of her own home.

"I have a security system," she said. "And I'll use it."

Dutton muttered some profanity under his breath. "Then I'll be there to keep watch to make sure the killer doesn't get to you."

She muttered her own profanity. "Dutton, there is no way I can let you stay with me in my house."

"I'll stay in my truck, which will be parked in front of your house," he argued.

He would have no doubt continued to argue if her phone hadn't dinged with a text, and she saw it was from Larry. As promised, the CSI had sent her a photo of the knife they'd found. It was now encased in a clear plastic evidence bag, but she could see the smears of blood on the blade, and Grace felt the fresh punch of dread since this was the blood of a fallen fellow cop.

"Enlarge the handle," Dutton insisted.

Of course, she was aware he'd moved back to her side. It was impossible not to realize that since…well, this was Dutton. But Grace heard something in his voice that was more than a request.

She used her fingers to enlarge the photo, zooming in on the handle. It was ornate, alright, and made of something white. Maybe a special kind of wood or bone. An eagle had been carved into it.

"Hell," Dutton said, and he groaned, then cursed some more.

Grace snapped toward him to see why he'd had that reaction. "What's wrong?" she demanded.

Dutton groaned again before he answered. "That knife belongs to my father."

Chapter Four

"Won't this be fun?" Dutton muttered, the sarcasm heavy in his voice. He was in the doorway of Grace's office and had an unobstructed view of his father as Ike came into the police station.

Grace, who was right beside Dutton, didn't say anything, but her sigh told him she wasn't looking forward to this, either. Her sigh turned to a raised eyebrow though when an unexpected *visitor* came in behind Ike. Dutton cursed under his breath at the sight of the dark-haired girl.

His twelve-year-old cousin, Jamie.

The girl's arrival obviously grabbed the attention of his brother, too, because Rory got up from his desk. He was talking to someone on the phone, but he pinned a questioning look at Ike and Jamie.

Dutton did more than give her a look. "What are you doing here, Jamie?" Dutton demanded. He checked his watch. It was one-fifteen in the morning, which was way past the girl's bedtime.

Jamie gave a dramatic roll of her eyes. "Dutton, Sheriff Granger," she greeted, and her attention lowered to Grace's baby bump.

The girl smiled a little. For some reason, Jamie was one of the few people in town who seemed happy about the pregnancy.

"Well?" Dutton persisted. "Why are you here?"

"I heard when the sheriff called and told Uncle Ike to come into the station. I insisted on coming with him."

"Insisted," Ike snarled, not sounding too pleased at having a companion for this. Then again, his father was likely just riled at pretty much everything that had gone on tonight.

Dutton ignored Ike for the time being and focused on Jamie. "Does your nanny know you're here?" he asked.

"No, she's asleep, and please don't call her," Jamie was quick to say. When Dutton took out his phone to do just that, the girl added, "Sheriff Granger, I can help with the investigation."

Grace pulled back her shoulders, and Dutton moved to the side so that Grace could come out of her office and walk closer to Jamie. Dutton followed her. "What investigation?" she asked, aiming a glare at Ike for spilling any info about a murder to a child.

"I didn't say a word," Ike protested.

"He didn't have to," Jamie explained. "It's all over social media about the woman who was left by the fence."

Of course, it was, and Dutton didn't press to know why Jamie would have read such things. He already knew. Jamie's own parents had been murdered when she was a baby, and it was how she'd ended up in foster care and then adopted by his aunt and uncle.

Jamie's tragic family history had given her a fascination with police investigations. So much so that she'd applied to do a summer internship of sorts here at the police station. Grace might approve it, too, in a limited-scope kind of way with Jamie only getting schooled on procedures for nonserious cases.

Grace was clearly more tolerant of Jamie than she was

the rest of his family. Including him. And it was easy to see that Jamie idolized Grace.

"It's awful what happened to her," Jamie went on. "And it's like that other murder, isn't it?"

"I can't discuss that with you," Grace said, probably hoping that was the last of the conversation about murder. "You really shouldn't be here."

"But I had to come. Like I said, I can help," Jamie insisted, and she was no doubt about to add more when her eyes lit up. "Sherlock," she called out as the cat waltzed toward her.

Dutton knew that Jamie was familiar with the cat because she'd gone with Rory when he'd taken Sherlock in for a checkup with the vet. Jamie scooped him up, and the often standoffish cat consented to some cuddles.

"Help how?" Grace pressed the girl.

"I know about the knife," Jamie stated.

Everything inside Dutton went still. Hell. He didn't want Jamie involved in this in any way, but if what she said was true, then her involvement was already there.

"Like I said, I heard when Sheriff Granger called Uncle Ike," Jamie continued a moment later. "He didn't put the call on speaker or anything, but I could tell from the way he was answering that the sheriff was asking him about that knife with the white handle he keeps in his office. Not locked up," she added. "But sitting in a little wooden holder on the top of the big bookshelf behind his desk."

That was indeed where his father had kept it, and it had been there for as long as Dutton could remember. It was way out of reach of kids and was surrounded by other antique memorabilia. Dutton hadn't been in that office in more than a year, and even if he had had a more recent visit, he likely wouldn't have noticed it was missing.

"A knife that isn't there because someone stole it," Ike snapped, his ire aimed at Grace, not Jamie. "And then that someone used it to try to set me up. I didn't kill that woman."

Grace sighed, obviously not comfortable discussing a murder in front of a child. "You said you knew something about the knife?" she reminded Jamie.

Jamie nodded. "Last month when I was home on spring break, this electrician came. He claimed that he needed to check some wiring, and he had some kind of ID from the electrical company that must have been convincing enough because Miss Diane let him in."

Diane McGrath was the current head housekeeper at the ranch, and while Dutton didn't have daily contact with the woman, this was the first he was hearing about an electrician.

"I wasn't home when this happened," Ike said, taking up the explanation. "I was at a meeting in San Antonio. And Asher and Kitty were away on one of their usual trips."

He grumbled *usual* as if it was a profanity. Which it sort of was, in this case. Jamie's parents were gone far more than they were home and rarely took their daughter with them on their travels to tropical adults-only resorts. There were times Dutton wondered why they had adopted a child only to leave her in the care of a nanny.

"Was there something about this electrician that was suspicious?" Grace asked, aiming the question at Jamie.

"Definitely suspicious," Jamie said quickly. "I mean, he did more looking at the stuff in the house than he did the outlets and such. I thought he was casing the place. I was about to call Uncle Ike so he could check and make sure this guy was for real, but he up and left."

"Did you get his name and confirm he was actually

with the electric company? And do you believe he stole the knife?" Grace pressed.

Ike shook his head and grumbled something under his breath. "Diane doesn't remember the man's name. She said the ID looked real, though, and that she personally didn't follow him around to see where he went. She definitely didn't notice him going into my office. But he must have. He must have gone in and stolen it."

Grace stayed quiet a moment. "Alright, I'll contact the electric company and see if they sent anyone out."

"I'll do that," Rory volunteered. "Though there probably won't be anyone in their office for hours."

Grace muttered a thanks for Rory taking that chore, then turned back to Jamie. "Describe this man."

The girl's forehead bunched up as she continued to stroke a now purring Sherlock. "Reddish brown hair, but most of it was covered up by a cap. It had the electric company logo on it. I didn't get close enough to him to see the color of his eyes, but I think his beard might have been fake. It didn't look like it belonged on his face, if you know what I mean."

Jamie was certainly observant. And maybe overly suspicious as well. Since she'd said this had happened during her spring break, she might have been bored enough for her imagination to go way overboard. Dutton almost hoped that was the case because the alternative sickened him.

It meant the killer could have been in the house with Jamie.

Grace turned to Ike. "Is it possible your security system recorded the visit?" she asked.

Ike shook his head and looked at Dutton for the answer, but Jamie responded before he could. "Yes, but the feed records over itself after a week."

The sound Grace made indicated that was what she'd expected. "How tall was this man? And how was he built?" Grace continued.

"Shorter than Dutton and Rory." Jamie paused, obviously giving that more thought. "So maybe five-ten-ish. And he was on the skinny side." Her eyes brightened again. "Maybe I can work with a sketch artist."

"Possibly," Grace said. "But if he actually is or was an employee of the electric company, we should be able to get his name. Then, he can be brought in for questioning." And Grace would have another person of interest to add to her murder board.

"Questioning?" Ike said, using more of the irritated tone. "Like what you're doing to me right now. I didn't kill that woman," he stressed.

Grace drew in a long breath. "For the time being, I believe you," she stated, cutting off what would have no doubt been a continued tirade from him.

Dutton didn't know who was more surprised by Grace's comment, but he thought Ike won that particular prize. Still, he didn't seem willing to soften the hard look he was giving Grace.

"It's possible this is some kind of reverse psychology," she continued, ignoring Ike's expression. "But if you had committed this crime, I don't believe you would have used a knife that could be so easily traced back to you. And you wouldn't have left the bodies by the ranch. Everything points to someone setting you up. Or setting up someone in your family." She glanced at Rory and Jamie, and then Dutton.

Ike muttered something under his breath again. Probably a profanity that Dutton hoped Jamie hadn't heard. "Plenty of folks dislike me and my kin. But I see this going back to you." At the sound of the front door opening, they all turned and looked in that direction. "Or back to your kin," Ike snarled.

And Grace's mother, Aileen, came in.

Even though the woman was in her sixties now, she looked just as formidable as she did when she'd worn the badge, and she seemed to take in the entire room with her cop eyes. Eyes that were nearly identical to Grace's own. In fact, the two shared enough features that it was no mistaking they were related.

"Sorry for the interruption," Aileen said, settling her attention on her daughter. The apology seemed heartfelt. So was the look she gave Grace.

And Dutton.

Hell. What now?

Unlike many people in town, Aileen didn't seem to despise him simply because he was a McClennan. Though there wasn't exactly a warm, fuzzy feeling between them, either. Especially since he'd gotten Grace pregnant. But Dutton hadn't recalled Aileen ever giving him that sort of look. An apology mixed with something else.

Worry.

Aileen walked past Jamie and Ike, giving them a nod of greeting that conveyed zero warmth. Well, for Ike, anyway. Aileen's expression softened a little when she glanced at Jamie.

"I wouldn't have come if it weren't necessary," Aileen said to her daughter. "But someone sent me this." She held out her phone for Grace.

Grace took it and read what was on the screen. Dutton read it, too, and barely managed to bite off the profanity in front of Jamie.

"Your daughter and her lover will be dead soon," he read aloud.

"Unknown sender," Aileen explained. "Which means it'll likely be impossible to trace, but I figured you'd want to try."

Grace nodded, and while most people would have thought she appeared composed, Dutton saw the nerves in the slight tightening of her mouth. "Yes, I definitely want to try. I'll have it sent to the tech guys at the lab."

Rory whipped out an evidence bag and took Aileen's phone to get that process started. Dutton wasn't an expert on such things, but he was the brother of a cop and figured that an unknown sender would cover his or her tracks well enough so it couldn't be traced. Still, Grace might get lucky.

"Why would the killer want to involve you in this?" Dutton asked Aileen.

Aileen lifted her shoulder, and he saw the nerves in her expression, too. "Maybe because it'll put Grace under more pressure. Because now she's probably wondering if the killer will try to use me in some way to make her suffer even more." She locked eyes with Grace. "I'm retired, but I'm not careless. I'm taking precautions just as I'm sure you're doing. You, too," she added to Dutton.

"Precautions will be taken," Grace assured her.

Her mother studied her. And sighed. "You're going back to your place. Alone."

Grace nodded.

"And you can't talk her out of it," Aileen said to Dutton.

"I can't," he verified.

Aileen sighed again. "Alright, you can both stay at my place if you want. You could consider it Switzerland. Neutral territory."

There was nothing neutral about it because it belonged to a woman who had a feud going on with his family. Added to that, Dutton wasn't sure Aileen's house would be any safer than Grace's. It probably had a security system, but it, too, was out in the country and far away from any backup.

"Thank you for the offer, but no," Grace said. "I won't let the killer run me out of my own home."

Aileen looked at him, maybe to see if she thought there was anything he could do to change Grace's mind. There wasn't. And the look he gave Aileen must have conveyed that because she didn't press.

"Alright," Aileen said on a sigh. "Let me know when I can get my phone back." She handed Grace a yellow sticky note she took from her pocket. "That's the number of the burner I'll be using in the meantime."

Aileen muttered a goodbye, but didn't hug Grace. Though it looked as if that's what she wanted to do. But Aileen probably felt like any show of affection like that wasn't appropriate for the workplace. She gave all of them one last look before she headed back out into the night.

"Am I free to go, too?" his father snarled at Grace. "Or do you need to pester me with more questions?"

"You're free to go," she said. "And I'll see about getting the sketch artist," she added to Jamie.

Jamie smiled as if this was some grand adventure, but the smile quickly faded. "You two are going to be careful, right?" Jamie asked Grace and him. "I mean, you're not going to like make yourselves bait or anything like that?"

"We aren't," Grace and he said in unison.

That relieved a little of the fresh worry on the girl's face, and she set down the cat after giving him one last cuddle. Unlike Aileen, Jamie went with some PDA, first hugging Dutton, then Rory.

Then Grace.

Dutton had to hand it to Grace. She didn't protest the

gesture. She just went with it, and murmured, "Everything will be alright."

Of course, there was no way Grace could be sure. The killer didn't seem to be backing off, and that text to Aileen proved it.

"You need to be careful," Dutton told his father.

Ike opened his mouth as if to argue that but then closed it. Nodded. "You, too. I'll change the codes on the security system just in case that so-called electrician tries to get back in."

Dutton nodded in approval and then watched as his dad and Jamie headed out. He glanced at his brother, who was still on the phone, probably trying to get in touch with someone from the electric company. Then, Dutton turned to Grace to try once again to convince her to stay either with him or at her mother's. However, her landline rang before he had a chance to say a word.

"It's Dispatch," she muttered when she saw the blinking light on the base of the phone. She immediately went into her office to answer it.

And Dutton held his breath. Hell. He hoped there hadn't already been another murder. Rory must have thought that was a possibility, too, because he ended his call and joined Dutton in the office doorway.

"Sheriff Granger," she answered, and thankfully she put the call on speaker.

"You have a call from a Felicity Martinez," the dispatcher informed Grace. "She says she has information about the murder."

Grace looked up at Dutton and Rory to see if they recognized the name, but they both shook their heads. His brother and he also started searches on their phones.

"Put the call through," Grace instructed, and moments later, Dutton heard the woman come onto the line.

"Sheriff Granger," she said, and there was a tremble in her voice.

"Yes. How can I help you, Miss Martinez?" Grace asked.

"I, uh…" She stopped, and Dutton heard the woman's sob. "I've been seeing Brian Waterman."

Dutton had no trouble recalling who that was. Elaine's fiancé.

"Seeing?" Grace queried.

Another sob. "I've been having an affair with him. And, yes, I know he's engaged. He was up-front about that but said he couldn't break up with her, that it'd crush her parents if he didn't go through with it, that they would probably even fire him since he works for them."

Dutton figured that Grace had only scratched the surface of her research on Brian, and an affair might not have come out in the usual background checks.

"I'm the other woman," Felicity muttered. "I know it was wrong, but I'm in love with him. Was in love with him," she amended.

Grace jumped right on that. "Was? What happened to change your feelings about him?"

Felicity couldn't answer for a couple of seconds because she was sobbing more now. "Brian called me about an hour ago and said he needed for me to tell the cops that he was with me tonight. He said I was to say we're old friends and we were just catching up and that he was telling me all about his wonderful fiancée."

Grace's expression went hard. "Was Brian with you tonight?"

"No," Felicity said on another sob. "I haven't seen him in two weeks." She paused. "And then I heard on the news about the woman who was murdered. It was her, wasn't it? Brian's fiancée?"

Grace didn't answer those questions. "Where was Brian when he called you?"

"He wouldn't say, but I assumed he was at his house in San Antonio. I'm in Austin, and it's not storming here, but I could hear thundering in the background when I was talking to him."

Or the man could have been in Renegade Canyon, since San Antonio was less than an hour away.

"Has Brian been to El Paso any time over the past week?" Grace asked, obviously following up on what the man had told the police.

"No. Not that I know of." She stopped, and Dutton could hear her trying to slow down her breathing. She failed. "And he wouldn't explain why he needed me to lie to the cops." Felicity broke down again. "Sheriff Granger, I just have to know. Did Brian murder his fiancée?"

Chapter Five

Did Brian murder his fiancée?

That was the question that kept repeating through Grace's head. Too bad she didn't have an answer, but she hoped to remedy that soon.

First, though, she had to locate Brian, and so far she wasn't having any luck. He hadn't responded to a knock on the door when officers from San Antonio PD had gone to his house. So Grace had left messages for him not only on his personal phone, but also with his employer. If she didn't hear from the man soon, she would need to issue an APB. With Brian's alibi in question and asking his lover to lie for him, Grace had grounds to force him to come in for questioning.

The second thing going through her mind was Dutton. Even when the man was out of sight, it was hard to keep her thoughts off him. It was impossible now that he was following her in his truck.

She had no doubts—none—that he'd stick to his "threat" of sleeping outside her house. Sadly, part of her actually welcomed that for the sake of their baby's safety, but she also didn't want Dutton sitting in his vehicle if the killer just decided to gun him down. She doubted he'd agree to sleep in the bullet-resistant cruiser, either.

And that left Grace with a huge dilemma.

She could back down on her insistence that he not stay with her. Or she could just accept it for what was left of this night. Then, after a few hours of sleep, she might be able to work out a better arrangement.

She turned onto the road that led to her place, and while she was always aware of her surroundings, she was more so right now. The rain had stopped, but there were still plenty of clouds to block out the moon, making it pitch-black. The headlights of her cruiser created some spooky-looking shadows as she drove past the trees and shrubs that lined the road. She hoped one of those shadows wasn't the killer, but she had to be prepared just in case.

The house came into view, and she used the voice command on her phone app to turn on not only the porch lights, but also the ones on both floors of her house. Gone was the absolute darkness, but not the shadows, and she slowed, looking for any signs of an attack.

Nothing.

Since the house was well over a hundred years old, there was no garage, but she pulled beneath the covered part of her driveway that was only steps away from the door that led into the kitchen. Of course, Dutton pulled in right behind her, and he was darn fast at getting out of his truck.

"I want to check the house," he insisted. "To make sure no one got in."

She didn't remind him that she had a security system that would have alerted her to an intruder. That's because Grace knew systems could be hacked.

So far, the killer hadn't used something like that to get to the victims. There'd been no break-ins at either woman's residence. Instead, they'd likely been snatched shortly after leaving work and incapacitated in some way. In the case of the first murder, that had been with a stun gun, and Grace was betting the same had happened to Deputy Elaine Sneed.

And that brought her to a big question.

How had the killer gotten so close to two cops to use a stun gun on them? If Brian was indeed responsible, then getting close to Elaine wouldn't have been a problem since they were engaged. But what about the first cop? Grace needed to look for a possible connection there. First, though, she had to do some looking around her house.

Again, using the app, she unlocked her kitchen door and moved quickly inside. Dutton was right behind her, and it didn't surprise her when he drew a gun from the back waist of his jeans. He had a permit to carry a concealed weapon and Grace knew he wouldn't hesitate to use the weapon to protect her. Even if she was capable of protecting herself.

She drew her own gun, and without speaking, they started the room-to-room search. First, the bottom floor. The kitchen, then the living area, her office and the small bathroom that she'd had added after she'd moved in a decade earlier.

Dutton made it to the stairs a split second ahead of her, which meant she ended up following him. Something she didn't care for on several levels. First, she didn't want him in the lead here, and second, she didn't appreciate the view she had of his rather superior backside.

Well, she actually did appreciate it.

Her body did, anyway. But it was a reminder and a distraction she didn't need. It didn't help that the rest of his body fell into that superior category as well, and once again, she silently cursed this need for him that just wouldn't go away.

They searched the three upstairs bedrooms, including

the empty one she'd had cleared out for the nursery. Soon, it would be painted a pale yellow, since Grace hadn't planned on learning the gender of the baby before delivery. Some considered that an old-fashioned notion, but she was trying to savor every moment of this pregnancy since it would likely be her one and only.

And it was somewhat of a miracle.

Over the years, doctors had told her it would be hard for her to conceive because of irregular ovulation, but Grace had figured she would still try if she fell in love and married. That hadn't happened, and now with her thirty-eighth birthday on the horizon, she had all but given up on the possibility of motherhood.

That one night with Dutton had changed everything.

And Grace was fighting to hold on to some kind of control and normalcy in her life. This murder investigation and the close contact with Dutton weren't going to help with that. But somehow, she had to keep her feelings for him at bay. If not, they could both pay a very high price by giving the killer a window to get to them.

After finishing the room search, he went to the top of the stairs and frowned when he looked out the massive window over the front door. Dutton quickly switched off the lights. Grace didn't have to ask why. Usually, that window gave her an amazing view of the pastures and the six horses she owned. But now, she was very much aware that it would give the killer a clear line of sight of her whenever she went up or down the stairs.

"Is anything out of place?" Dutton asked, drawing her attention back to him. Not that it'd strayed too far. "Any sense that anyone has been in here?"

"No." And that was the truth. Still, her nerves were far from being steady. "I can keep the lights off up here on the stairwell and in the hall. Or I can sleep downstairs. My office has a pullout sofa."

Still frowning, Dutton turned to her. "You've dug in your heels about me not staying here with you?"

She nodded, though Grace had to admit her heels didn't feel as firmly dug in as they had earlier. That wasn't just for her sake, either. Or the baby's. "You've dug in your heels about keeping watch of the place?"

His nod was a lot firmer than hers had been.

Grace sighed. "Then will you at least stay in the cruiser?"

The corners of his mouth lifted in a smile that made his face even hotter than usual. "Yes." Their gazes connected and held for a few moments before the smile faded. "And will you stay away from the windows?"

She made a sound of agreement. No security system would prevent someone from shooting through the glass. And that brought her right back to Dutton. The windows of the cruiser were bullet-resistant, but that didn't mean it was a safe place to spend the night. Grace was about to press him once again to return home to his ranch when she saw the movement out the large window.

"Hell," Dutton muttered, and he'd obviously seen it, too.

A woman wearing a billowing white dress was staggering through the darkness toward Grace's house. Once again, Dutton beat her to the punch and hurried down the stairs ahead of her. She was about to warn him not to open the door, but that wasn't necessary. Dutton slapped off the lights in the entry and went to the front window instead. He kept to the side and peered out.

She turned off some lights, too, on her way to the window to join him, but she kept the porch light on so they'd be able to see if the approaching woman was armed. Grace took up position on the opposite side of the window from Dutton, and both of them kept their guns drawn and ready.

"She's got blood on her dress," Dutton muttered.

Grace could see that. Not a lot of it, but there were streaks running down the sides of her dress.

"But I don't know who she is. Do you?" he asked.

"No." The woman with the long, dark brown hair, a lanky body and an ashen face was a stranger.

Grace felt that punch of dread that went well beyond just worry and concern. Was this another potential victim who'd managed to escape?

Or was this a trap?

The woman truly did appear to be injured, but that could all be a facade meant to draw them out. In fact, this could be the killer, someone who hadn't even been a suspect in the investigation.

"Help me," Grace heard the woman yell as she neared the house.

"Don't open the door yet," Grace instructed Dutton, even though he didn't look anywhere ready to do that. No doubt because he, too, was concerned this might be some kind of ploy to kill them.

Grace took out her phone to call for both backup and an ambulance. If the woman was truly hurt, then she would need help. And if she was the killer, then Grace wanted at least one of her deputies here to assist with the takedown and the arrest. Also, in case this turned into a full-fledged attack.

They watched as the woman made it to the porch steps. She didn't look in the window, where she might have spotted Dutton and Grace. Her eyes seemed unfocused, but her attention remained on the door.

She didn't make it.

The woman stumbled and fell face-first onto the porch. Her head hit hard, loud enough for the sound of the thud to carry into the house, and she didn't move. She just lay there, sprawled out over the steps.

"Backup and the ambulance are ten minutes out," Grace reported when she got the text of the update. Considering she lived six miles out of town and on a rural road, that was fast.

But maybe not fast enough.

Grace felt an overwhelming sense of dread as she stood there and saw the blood begin to pool around the woman's head. "I have to go out there," she said.

"I'll go," Dutton quickly volunteered. "I can carry her inside—"

She was shaking her head before he finished. "And while you're carrying her, you wouldn't be able to return fire if someone tries to kill you. There's a real possibility of that," she added. "The killer could have drugged the woman and pointed her here toward my house just to get us to open the door."

In a perfect scenario, Grace would be able to handle this on her own. But this wasn't perfect. She couldn't lift the woman by herself. So she either had to wait the fifteen minutes for the ambulance and backup…

Or she had to accept Dutton's help.

She glanced at the bleeding, unconscious woman again and knew what she had to do. "Please feel free to say no to any part of this rescue plan," she stated.

"Depends on the plan," he replied right back. "If it involves putting the baby at risk, then the plan isn't going to happen."

Grace figured he'd said "the baby" instead of "you" on purpose, to remind her of just how dangerous this could be. "I can't make this risk-free," she argued. She tapped her badge. "But I can't stand by and not offer someone assistance when she could be out there dying."

Dutton stared at her. And then he cursed. His groan told her what she already knew. Even without a badge, Dutton would help someone in need, and at the moment, the need was there. If it turned out the woman was the killer, then an arrest could put an end to the danger. No more female cops would die, and she and Dutton could get back to their normal lives.

Well, as normal as things could be for them, anyway.

"We need to do this fast," Grace said, hoping that by spelling it out, she would figure out a way to make this safer for both of them. "We both stay down and go out on the porch. We'll check to make sure she isn't armed. If she is, I disarm her. If she isn't, you can bring her inside while I cover you."

She could tell Dutton wasn't a fan of what she was proposing, but he nodded. "Any chance you have a Kevlar vest around you can use?"

"There's one in the trunk of the cruiser." Which meant trying to get it was out of the question since it would mean going outside to retrieve it. It would be faster just to rescue the woman.

Dutton cursed again and met her gaze head-on for a couple of seconds before he headed toward the door. "Stay down, and on the count of three…"

Grace nodded and temporarily disarmed her security system while she went to the door. Dutton didn't hesitate on doing the countdown. Nor did he wait once he'd reached three. He unlocked the door and threw it open.

The night air rushed in. It was damp and earthy from the storm. But there was also the smell of blood. Grace prayed the woman wasn't already dead. Even if she was the killer, Grace wanted her alive so she could answer so many questions.

Grace glanced around the yard and the road. No sign of anyone. Of course, that didn't mean someone wasn't there, waiting to try to get the best shot possible at Dutton and her.

Together, they rushed onto the porch, and both of them kept watch while Dutton frisked the woman as best he could. "I can't find a weapon," he said, scooping her up into his arms.

The woman moaned, the sound of someone in pain. Or perhaps someone pretending to be. But one thing was for certain—the blood was real. So was the injury on her head, probably from where she'd fallen.

Moving the woman was risky. However, staying put was riskier. If the murderer was indeed out there, the woman could be killed.

"In the house," Dutton insisted, firing a quick glance at Grace.

But Grace held her ground and waited so she could continue to cover him until he was inside. Grace's lungs were aching, but she finally released the breath she'd been holding once she was in the foyer and had locked the door.

"Search her again for weapons," she instructed once Dutton had laid the woman on the floor. Grace watched him do that while she rearmed the security system.

Dutton patted her down, and then Grace repeated the procedure once she'd put away her phone. Not just a patdown, but she also checked to see the source of the bleeding. The woman wasn't armed. And those injuries were very much real. Not just the fresh one on her head, but now that Grace had gotten a closer look, she could see the cuts in the fabric on the front of the woman's dress.

She'd been stabbed.

Grace handed Dutton her phone. "Check on the status of the ambulance." Now that her hands were free, she balled up the front of the woman's dress and used it to apply pressure to the wounds. There were at least two cuts, maybe more. It didn't appear she was on the verge of bleeding out, but there could be serious or even fatal internal injuries.

Beside her, Dutton called Dispatch, and he'd just gotten through when a crashing sound tore through the house. Breaking glass.

Mercy. The noise caused Grace's heart to drop to her knees. What had happened? It sounded like a window had been broken, which meant that someone could be trying to break in.

Before Grace could try to pinpoint the location of the sound, the alarm kicked on. Not a warning beep, either. This was a full-blown blaring that drowned out all other sounds.

And then, Grace caught a whiff of something in the air.

A whiff that caused her eyes and throat to burn like fire. She couldn't breathe, and her instinct was to run. She didn't. Instead, she somehow managed to take her phone from Dutton and disable the alarm. A necessity to be able to hear someone approaching.

"Pepper spray," Dutton said, and he began to cough. So did Grace, and the woman on the floor was gasping for air as well.

Yes, this was most likely pepper spray, and while Grace had never been personally exposed to it, she had gone through training on how to deal with it. The spray hadn't actually come in contact with their skin, but it was obviously airborne, which meant it had likely been tossed or shot through the window.

It was next to impossible for Grace to see with her eyes

watering and burning, but she tried to think of what to do. Opening the door would allow in some fresh air. It could also allow the killer easy access.

"The bathroom," she blurted in between the coughs that were robbing her of every bit of her breath.

The door to that particular room was closed, and while it didn't have an exterior window, it did have a shower, and right now, she thought that was their best bet in washing the pepper spray from their eyes.

Despite the coughing, Dutton managed to pick up the woman, and they stumbled their way to the bathroom. They got inside as fast as they could and locked the door.

Grace tried to drag in as much of the fresh air as she could while groping toward the shower. She tried not to think of what this might be doing to her baby. Or if the killer was about to break down the door and come after them. She just focused on turning on the shower.

Dutton lay the woman on the floor and shoved the bath mat against the bottom of the door to stop the pepper spray from seeping in. He also wet the hand towel in the sink and placed it over the woman's eyes.

Grace dropped her phone and her gun on the closed toilet lid, where they would hopefully be easy to reach if someone did try to knock down the door, and she stepped into the shower. Dutton didn't follow her, maybe because he wanted to be able to hold on to his gun. Instead, he ducked his head beneath the running faucet in the sink. Hopefully, they'd be able to get their vision cleared before the killer could come after them.

Well, maybe that was the killer's plan.

Grace didn't know if that was it, or if this wounded woman somehow played into things. She hoped she got the chance to find out before any more damage was done.

She kept her eyes closed but held her face up to the spray of water. Within seconds, Grace felt some relief, though her eyes weren't anywhere near normal just yet. So she stayed under the water, blinking hard, trying to wash away the burning sensations caused by the pepper spray.

Outside, Grace heard the welcome sound of sirens, and she prayed the EMTs and her deputies weren't walking into a trap. Dutton must have considered the same thing because he came out from beneath the running water long enough to call Dispatch.

"This is Dutton McClennan," he said. "Alert the responders to the sheriff's house that there could be an attacker lying in wait."

Grace immediately had a sickening thought. She had two female deputies, and if one of them was a responder, then she could be the target. This could have all been set up to kill another cop.

She came out of the shower, the water still sliding down her face and the rest of her. She was soaked to the bone, but she took her phone from Dutton and ended the call with the dispatcher, then called Rory, since she knew he was on duty and would no doubt be in the cruiser that was approaching her house.

"What happened?" Rory asked the moment he was on the line, and Grace put the call on speaker so Dutton could hear what was being said.

"An injured woman came to the house, and then someone fired pepper spray through the window," Grace explained. "Who's with you?" she quickly asked.

Rory was equally quick with his answer. "Livvy."

Grace groaned. No. Not this. Not one of her own. "Livvy stays in the cruiser, understand?"

"No—" Rory began, but then he stopped. "Livvy's the target?"

"Possibly. Is anyone else responding?"

"Judson and Bennie," he said, referring to Deputies Judson Docherty and Bennie Whitt.

Grace's next breath was one of relief. Until she considered something else. "Call Eden and make sure she's okay."

Rory cursed, and the alarm deepened in his voice. With good reason. Deputy Eden Gallagher was Rory's ex, and she was also the mother of his son. And Eden could be the target, not Livvy or her. The best way to torture and punish Grace would be to go after one of her people.

Grace ended the call with Rory so he could contact Eden, and while she waited, she looked at Dutton. His eyes were red and his skin was flushed, but he seemed to be able to focus. He also had his gun drawn and was keeping watch of the door. Grace picked up her gun and did the same while she also checked on the woman.

Still alive, but there was a lot of blood on her dress.

"Sheriff Granger?" someone called out. It was Judson, which meant Bennie was close behind.

"Here," she answered.

She heard both the deputies coughing, no doubt reacting to the still lingering pepper spray, and a moment later there was a knock at the bathroom door. Dutton opened it, slowly and cautiously. Maybe because he thought there was a possibility the killer had taken the deputies hostage.

Thankfully, that hadn't happened, and the moment Dutton had the door fully open, she saw Judson do a sweeping glance around the bathroom while Bennie kept watch behind him.

"Are you all okay?" Judson asked.

No. Grace was far from okay, but she nodded, anyway.

She wasn't injured, but there was still the fear of the effects this was having on the baby. The fear, too, that this attack wasn't over.

"The ambulance just arrived," Judson explained. "I'll get the EMTs in here." He fired off a quick text to do that, and then he looked at Grace. It was the kind of look that told her something else was wrong.

"What is it?" she asked. "What happened?" And she forced herself to tamp down the worst-case scenarios flying through her head.

"There's a note on the front door," Judson explained, and then he paused. "I think it's written in blood."

Chapter Six

Look how easy it is to get to you, Grace. This was a trial run. Next time, it'll be the real thing.

Dutton had an image of the note fixed in his head. The note that had been taped to the front door, right here at Grace's house. And Judson had indeed been right.

It'd been written in blood.

Whose blood was still to be determined, but it'd been sent to the lab for analysis. Dutton assumed it belonged to the injured woman who had collapsed on Grace's porch. A woman who, the last he heard, was clinging to life.

All of that—the pepper-spray attack, the injured woman, the threatening note, the other two dead cops—hadn't allowed him to get much sleep. Then again, he hadn't expected to get much sleep, anyway.

Not since he was staying under the same roof with Grace.

They weren't at her house, though, since it would need to be processed as a crime scene as well as have the window replaced. That's why they had ended up at Rory's house with Grace and Dutton in guestrooms directly across from each other. And sharing a bathroom. His body hadn't let him forget that.

At least the pepper spray hadn't harmed the baby. Grace and he knew that because she'd gone to the hospital shortly after the attack and had a checkup along with an ultrasound. All was well with their child. In the grand scheme of things, that was a top priority, and now Dutton had to figure out how to keep them safe when Grace was trying to do the same to him.

He checked the time—almost seven, which meant he'd been taking catnaps on and off for the past four hours. Maybe Grace was faring better across the hall, and that's why Dutton stayed as quiet as possible when he made his way to the bathroom. He took a quick shower and changed into the clean clothes that he'd had one of his ranch hands bring over shortly after they'd arrived at Rory's. Dutton was still zipping up his jeans as he came out of the bathroom.

And ran right into Grace.

Thankfully, not a hard slam, but there was body-to-body contact. Contact he was even more aware of since he hadn't buttoned his shirt. She'd put up her hand on impact, and it landed against his bare chest.

"Sorry," she said and stepped back as if he'd scalded her.

Dutton instantly felt the loss of the contact. Probably because he'd instantly felt it in every inch of his body. Not good. He didn't need this physical ache for her playing into, well, anything. Still, the ache came, anyway. So did the worry. Along with still managing to look amazing, the fatigue was there in her eyes.

"I was hoping you'd sleep in," he said.

She shook her head. "The baby's kicking."

That shifted his focus, and he wanted to put his hand on her stomach, wanted to feel those kicks. He didn't, though. And Grace didn't invite him to do it, so he stepped out of the bathroom to let her enter.

"Rory's in the kitchen," she informed him. "There have been a few updates, and he can fill you in."

Since Dutton very much wanted to hear any updates, he finished dressing, put on his boots, holstered his gun and made his way downstairs.

Unlike Grace's house, his brother's was only a few years old, and it had that new, modern feel to it. It was also closer to town, even though it was still out in the country, and like Dutton and the rest of the McClennans, Rory kept up the family tradition of raising horses. Rory had obviously shucked another tradition, though, by becoming a cop.

Dutton spotted two palominos out the side window that faced the pasture. He also spotted plenty of toys and a mesh playpen, a reminder that Rory was the father of a baby boy, Tyler, who wasn't quite one year old. Rory and the baby's mother, Eden, were estranged, but apparently they were managing to co-parent. Dutton was hoping Grace and he would be able to manage the same.

He followed the scent of coffee and found Rory in the kitchen, scrambling some eggs and frying some bacon. Rory took one look at Dutton and poured him a huge cup of the coffee. "Good thing you take it black because I'm out of sugar and milk."

"Thanks," Dutton said and took a sip. It was too hot, but he needed the caffeine hit. Needed to say something to his brother as well. "Thanks for letting us stay here last night."

His brother shrugged. "Anytime." He studied Dutton from over the rim of his own mug. "But I'm guessing you would have preferred to take Grace to your place at the ranch?"

Dutton made a sound of agreement. "This was a good compromise."

Rory's home had a security system along with a reserve deputy sitting in a cruiser out front. Dutton figured the killer wasn't bold enough to try to tape any notes written in blood on Rory's door with a cop watching and two more cops inside.

"Grace said you have some updates," Dutton prompted while he continued to gulp more coffee.

"Lots," Rory acknowledged. Some toast popped up from the toaster, and he put the two slices on a plate and set them on the counter next to Dutton. "The injured woman has been identified as Georgia Tate. She's in critical condition and unconscious so we haven't been able to question her."

"How'd you get an ID so fast?" Dutton asked while he ate some toast. He wasn't hungry, but his body needed fuel, and that was probably why his brother added some of the eggs and bacon to the plate. "Did she have a police record?"

"No, her sister filed a missing-person report on her. Georgia works in San Antonio, but she shares a house with her sister about ten miles from here, in Comanche Creek. She's employed as a cocktail waitress, and when she didn't come home after work, her sister filed the report. Good thing, too. Since there's no minimum period for filing a report in Texas, it helped us make a quick ID."

Dutton took a moment to process that. "Does Georgia have any obvious connection to Renegade Canyon or to Grace?"

"None that we've found so far, but Eden's working on it."

At the mention of the deputy's name, Dutton had to ask. "Are Eden and Tyler alright?"

A muscle flickered in Rory's jaw. "They're safe. Eden wouldn't stay here," he added. "But Livvy is at her place, and they have a reserve deputy outside in a cruiser as well."

Good. Livvy was a solid deputy. And possibly a target, too, since she was female. This way, Eden and Livvy could look after each other. But Dutton totally understood his brother's tight-jawed reaction. Rory would have preferred having his ex and son with him.

"A rep for the electric company came in early to check their records," Rory continued a moment later, obviously returning to the updates. "And they didn't send anyone to the ranch."

So that was bogus, which could mean a couple of things. Either the person was the actual killer, and the ploy was to steal the knife. Or the killer could have hired someone to go in. Either was possible, but it still didn't make sense to Dutton that the killer would use Ike's knife.

"Yeah," Rory said, and he was watching Dutton. "You're trying to work out what's going on with that knife. Maybe the killer didn't think Dad would have alibis?"

Dutton nodded. "Or else this is a way of creating bad publicity. Some stress, too. Because now the ranch and the family are part of the investigation."

Which pointed right back to Grace and him being the primary targets. It was possible the other murders had simply been meant to create more of that stress Dutton had just mentioned. But there was another possibility.

"What about the lying, cheating fiancé, Brian Waterman?" Dutton asked. "Any sign of him yet?"

"None, but there's an APB out on him now."

That was the right call because it was possible Brian was the person killing the female cops. Maybe all in an effort to cover up the murder of his own fiancée and to take the focus off him. But as far as Dutton was concerned, the focus was there, especially since Brian had seemingly dropped off the radar.

Dutton turned at the sound of footsteps, and as expected, Grace came in. Somehow, she'd managed to make herself look rested and ready for work. If he didn't look her straight in the eyes, that is. But he did, and saw the fatigue and the pressure this investigation had caused. Yet even that didn't lessen the reminder that she was a beautiful woman, and once again, he felt that usual kick of heat.

"Can your stomach handle some food?" Rory asked, fortunately interrupting the fantasy that Dutton was starting to spin about Grace.

She nodded. "Thankfully, the morning sickness passed a few weeks ago."

Dutton had known about the morning sickness, and he'd wished it was an ailment he could have taken on for her. Grace was bearing a lot of the downsides from this pregnancy. Then again, she was also getting the upside of feeling those kicks.

Rory dished her up a plate of the eggs, bacon and toast, but instead of coffee, she had a glass of water. Dutton wasn't sure how she managed to get through a morning without coffee, another downside to being pregnant.

"Thanks," she told Rory, and she sat at the counter to eat. "I just got an update from the CSIs," she said, tipping her head to her phone, which she set next to her plate. "There were no prints on the pepper-spray canister that was shot through the kitchen window. They believe it was probably launched with something like a paintball gun."

Dutton shook his head. "I didn't know that was possible."

"Neither did I," Grace admitted. "But this means almost anyone could have obtained a paintball gun and fired the shot. And apparently the shooter didn't even have to be that accurate, since there was a second canister that must have missed the window because the CSIs found it on the ground. It hit the side of the house."

So not a marksman. Well, maybe not. A lot of things could cause a person to miss a single shot. The other one had certainly been effective enough in getting them to take cover in the bathroom, which had likely been when their attacker had put that bloody note on the door.

"How about the note itself?" Dutton asked. "Anything on that yet?"

She nodded. "It's Elaine Sneed's blood."

Dutton silently cursed. What a sick SOB to hold on to one of the victim's blood to use it to write a message to Grace. This wasn't exactly breakfast conversation, but Grace continued with both the explanation and her breakfast.

"The paper is from a standard notebook you can buy anywhere, and the handwriting likely won't be able to be analyzed because it's smeared block lettering. Still, they'll send it to the lab."

"What about the tape?" Dutton asked. "Were there any fibers or prints on it? Any way to trace it to the source? And there must have been footprints or tire tracks somewhere because the ground was muddy."

Grace looked at him, lifted an eyebrow. "Have I told you before that you can sometimes sound like a cop?" Her mouth quivered in what might have been a suppressed smile.

Since this was probably as light of a moment as Grace and he were likely to have for a while, Dutton made a show of being insulted. "A momentary lapse." And he did smile. But as expected, it was short-lived.

Grace sighed. "No fibers or prints on the tape, and like the paper, it's the stuff you can buy pretty much anywhere." She sipped some water before she went on. "No tire tracks, which means the person either parked on the road or a trail and then walked to the house."

Dutton was going with option two. There were plenty of trails threading off the roads and into the woods, and even some of the pastures. Since these murders had started a month ago, that would have given the killer time to case Grace's house and property and know where to park in order to remain out of sight.

"There are some footprints," Grace confirmed, "but the person dragged their feet, no doubt to obscure them. It worked," she added in a disappointed mutter.

This was more proof they were dealing with someone who'd planned this to a *T*. And it'd worked. Well, maybe it had if the goal had been to terrorize them and put that note on the door. But if the killer had hoped to get into the house and go after them directly, then that had failed.

"Eden and I are digging into Georgia's background," Rory volunteered. "If we find out how and why she was taken, we might be able to figure out the who."

Grace made a sound of agreement. "Her doctor is supposed to contact us the moment she wakes up."

None of them voiced the worst-case scenario here. That Georgia might never wake up. That she could die from her injuries. If so, that would be three deaths, which would make the snake after them a serial killer.

"Any indications that Georgia was ever a cop or was maybe married to one?" Grace asked Rory.

Rory shook his head. "The best I could find was her brother-in-law was once a security specialist in the military."

Grace made another of those disappointed sighs, and Dutton decided he'd get his PI to do some digging on Georgia as well. It was possible the attack against her had been random, but there could be a reason the killer had chosen her. But then something occurred to Dutton.

Something that had him making one of those disappointed sighs.

"Georgia is alive," Dutton stated. "Yes, she was barely conscious when she made it to the house, but she had the chance to say something to help rat out the killer. She didn't."

Grace obviously knew where he was going with this. "So the killer probably concealed his or her identity. We might still be able to get something from Georgia, though. Height, weight, that sort of thing." But she didn't sound especially hopeful about that.

Dutton had to agree. Georgia had likely been drugged or stunned before she'd been taken, and then stabbed. He was still considering that when the sound of Grace's phone ringing shot through the room.

"It's Livvy," she told them, then she answered the call on speaker.

"Eden and I are at the station," Livvy immediately said. "And we have Tyler and his nanny here in the break room," she added, no doubt for Rory's benefit. "But someone just walked in and demanded to see you."

"Who?" Grace asked.

"Brian Waterman," Livvy replied. "And judging from his appearance, he's got a story to tell."

Grace was already getting to her feet. "What about his appearance?"

"There's blood all over the front of his shirt and on his hands," Livvy explained. "Lots and lots of blood."

Chapter Seven

With Rory in a second cruiser right behind her, Grace pulled into the parking lot of the police station. The reserve deputy was no longer with them and wouldn't return until night if needed.

Grace was very much hoping that it wouldn't be needed. But she steeled herself for that possibility, just in case.

She silently sighed because she'd already spent the last ten hours of her life in steeling-herself mode. First, for having Dutton so close to her at every waking moment—as he was at this very moment. Then, for dealing with the aftermath of the attack and murders. But now, the bracing herself and mental prep was for the man she was about to question.

Brian Waterman.

After Livvy had called to tell her that Brian had arrived at the police station, and that he was covered in blood, Grace hadn't pressed for any details other than to make sure Brian hadn't needed medical attention. Livvy had informed her that he had refused and had insisted on talking to her. Now that talk was about to happen, and it was possible she'd soon be making an arrest for the murders.

If Brian was here to confess, that is.

Grace hoped that was the reason for this impromptu visit and that his confession would explain why he had the blood on his clothes and hands. Maybe the explanation would include a lot of things, so it would put an end to the danger and this investigation. Then, there'd be a lot less *steeling up* required. For the threat of more murders.

For Dutton being around her.

Since threats included him, though, Grace intended to keep him in this pseudoprotective custody until the danger had passed. Of course, he was likely thinking the same thing about her. She knew he wanted her close so he could protect the baby and her, and at the moment, Grace had no intention of trying to talk him out of that.

"You could deputize me," Dutton said out of the blue.

She'd already reached for the handle of the cruiser door, but that stopped her. And for some reason, it made her smile. "Despite what I said about you sounding like a cop, you're not really cop material."

He smiled as well, causing dimples to flash in his cheeks. Yes, dimples. And somehow, they only managed to make that hot face of his even hotter. "True, but I could be in on the interviews if I had a badge. I could play bad cop and maybe get Brian to own up to the murders."

"I play bad cop." Or rather she had often taken on the tougher role in interviews before she'd gotten pregnant. The baby bump, though, had reduced any menacing presence she could bring into the room. "And I can't let you in interview. Everything I do has to hold up in case this goes to trial."

Dutton sighed, then nodded. And she saw the frustration in both actions. Frustration she understood because he wanted a quick end to this.

"I can let you observe," she conceded. "I can justify that by putting in my report that I wanted you to listen for anything that would connect you to the victims. Something that could explain why you were named as a target in the threatening note left on Elaine Sneed's body."

He nodded, accepting the compromise, and they got out of the cruiser and entered the building through the side entrance that led directly into her office. Rory was right behind them and went straight to his desk, where he no doubt had plenty of work waiting for him.

Grace immediately glanced around the bullpen and saw Livvy already making her way toward her. No sign of Brian, but Jamie, Eden and a woman whom Grace assumed was the sketch artist were huddled together around Eden's desk.

Jamie spotted them, too, and the girl gave a perky wave and smiled. Grace attempted a friendlier expression as well, but was sure she failed big-time. That's because of the somber look on Livvy's face.

"Where's Brian?" Grace asked the moment Livvy stepped into the office, and Grace noticed that the deputy looked both tired and wired. A common combination when an investigation was heating up.

"Interview room *A*," Livvy answered. "I stashed him there when I saw Jamie coming in to work with the sketch artist. I figured the kid didn't need to see someone in that state."

That was a good call. Jamie seemed much older than her years, but she was still just a child. A child who'd hopefully be able to give them a good enough likeness that they could use to identify the killer. If the sketch matched Brian, then that was even more evidence they'd have for an arrest.

"Brian refused medical treatment when I offered it again," Livvy went on, "but once I had him in the interview room and had read him his rights, he decided to do a little talking after all. He claimed he blacked out after drinking too much, and he woke up in a ditch. He let me take samples of the blood on his clothes, so I'm guessing it's actually his."

Dutton muttered some profanity, and Grace knew it was from disappointment. She was feeling it, too, because Livvy was right. Brian likely wouldn't have offered the sample if it had the potential to incriminate him.

The same could be said of his showing up at the police station like this. Then again, he might have done that to try to convince them that he'd been too drunk to kill his fiancée. It'd take more than that, though, to convince Grace of it.

"Observation," Grace reminded Dutton. "Livvy, you're with me in interview." And Grace was about to head that way when the front door opened, and Ike came in.

Her first instinct was to groan, that he was there to give her some grief, but then she realized he had come for Jamie. He made a beeline to the girl, and when he saw she was still working with the sketch artist, Ike turned his attention to Dutton and her.

"I need to tell you something," Ike said, aiming his statement at Grace.

So he might just dole out that grief after all.

Ike had his usual stony expression as he made his way toward them, but as he got closer, some of that look eased away. Grace thought he seemed almost hesitant. She was probably wrong about that, though. Ike McClennan wasn't the hesitating sort.

"I thought of something," he said, dodging Dutton's gaze and fixing his attention on Grace. "It's probably not important. But Cassie came to the ranch about two months ago."

Of all the things Grace had expected him to say, that wasn't one of them. And she latched right on to the timing. Two months ago was when her pregnancy had become public knowledge.

"What'd she want?" Dutton quickly asked.

"She wanted me to help her get back together with you," Ike admitted after a long pause, and he kept his voice at a whisper.

Dutton groaned and scrubbed his hand over his face. "I broke things off with Cassie a year ago," he said, and then he paused as well. And added some under-the-breath profanity. "Cassie was riled about me getting Grace pregnant."

Ike nodded. "Though riled is putting it mildly." He shifted his gaze to Dutton. "She was spitting mad and thought Grace had tricked you. She said it would ruin you financially if you two got together."

"We aren't together," Grace muttered just as Dutton insisted, "No trickery involved."

Dutton opened his mouth to say more but then stopped. Maybe because he was about to say the culprit was lust or something along those lines. Yes, best not to spell that out loud, especially since the lust was still lingering around.

"So what did she expect you to do to help her get back together with Dutton?" Grace asked Ike.

"She was short on specifics and long on ranting." Ike shook his head. "I think she just wanted to vent. She went on about how she'd always wanted kids and that Dutton didn't and that's why they broke up."

Dutton's next groan was laced with frustration. "I didn't want kids with her," he said and then sort of froze. Maybe because it sounded as if he didn't mind Grace being the mother of his child.

But Grace understood what he meant. She'd wanted kids, too, but she'd never found the right relationship for it. Then, when she'd gotten pregnant, she realized she could have the baby with no relationship commitment. Well, there was the whole co-parenting side, but that didn't mean she and Dutton had to be a couple.

"The reason I'm telling you all of this," Ike went on, "is because I'm thinking the knife could have been taken then."

Grace's heart rate revved up. "What do you mean?"

Ike huffed. "I mean Cassie could have taken it. We had the meeting in my office, and I had to step out for a couple of minutes to take an important call. When I came back in, Cassie was acting funny. Nervous and rattled, and she said a quick goodbye and hurried off."

"But you can't say for sure she took the knife," Grace concluded. It wasn't a question.

"No," Ike responded. "But she went from ranting to acting strange all within a matter of a couple of minutes. It's possible she took the knife, figuring she could use it somehow to get back at Dutton and you."

Grace played that all through. And felt a new wave of dread wash over her. Two months ago could have possibly been when the killer was plotting the murders. Of course, the plans could have happened well before that. And it didn't mean Cassie was the one doing the planning, or that she'd even been the one to take the knife, but Dutton's ex had to be questioned.

Feeling even more of that dread, she took out her phone and called Cassie's office. Almost immediately, Cassie's PA answered to say that Cassie wasn't in yet, so Grace left a message for the woman to come into the police station for a chat.

If Cassie didn't show soon, Grace would get the number for the woman's personal phone and try to contact her that way. She didn't think the woman was any kind of flight risk, so she wouldn't go full throttle on this now, especially since there was no proof that Cassie had taken the knife, only that she'd had the opportunity to do so.

"Thank you for letting me know," Grace told Ike.

He muttered something she didn't catch, but it definitely wasn't "you're welcome." There was still too much bitterness for that. It was possible Ike had held out hope of Dutton and Cassie getting back together, since Cassie was a much more palatable choice for Dutton than Grace would ever be. But Ike had come forward with this because he was also worried about Dutton's safety. If Cassie had indeed taken the knife, and was the killer, then Dutton was on her hit list.

And the woman had motive.

Even though Cassie had never ranted to Grace about her being pregnant with Dutton's baby, it was possible that Cassie was so enraged that she had crossed a very big line. She could be killing female cops to cover up that it was only one cop she wanted dead.

Grace.

She forced aside that troubling possibility and got back to work. She glanced at Jamie. Still busy with the sketch artist. So she motioned for Livvy and Dutton to follow her toward the interview with Brian. She showed Dutton into the observation area—not a room with a two-way mirror, but rather a computer where he'd be able to hear and see the interview.

Even though his observing was somewhat of a concession, Grace truly hoped he did hear something that would give them a clue as to why Brian might have targeted them. Of their two top suspects, she preferred Brian to be the killer, rather than Cassie. It was harder to accept when it was someone she knew who wanted Dutton and her dead.

Grace took in a couple of deep breaths before she stepped

into the interview room, and she got her first look at Brian. He was seated, his elbows on the metal table, and his hands bracketing the sides of his head. There was indeed blood on the front of his shirt, his hands, his jaw and even in his pale blond hair. She also saw a deep cut on his forehead and some scrapes and bruises on his arms and hands.

He immediately looked up, spearing her with eyes that were bloodshot. "Sheriff Granger?" he asked, getting to his feet.

She nodded and motioned for him to stay seated. "Were you read your rights, Mr. Waterman?" Grace asked.

She was certain he had been. However, she wanted both the question and his response on the recording that Livvy had started the moment they'd stepped into the room. Ditto for activating the camera mounted on the wall. A reminder that Dutton was watching every bit of this.

Brian pointed to Livvy. "She Mirandized me. But it wasn't necessary. There's been a big misunderstanding."

Grace had been a cop long enough to know that some suspects clammed up and some couldn't stop talking. She figured Brian was the latter because he continued as they took seats across from him.

"After I got the horrible news about Elaine, I got drunk." He shook his head as if disgusted with himself. "It's what I do. I drink when I'm stressed and when I can't deal. I just couldn't deal," he added, his voice cracking.

"Were you drinking at a bar or at home?" Grace asked. Because a bar would likely have security footage.

"Home," he said, dashing any notion of security footage. "When I got the call about Elaine, I walked around in a haze for a while. I was probably in shock. By the time I needed a drink, it was too late to go to a bar."

Grace kept her face blank. "Was anyone with you?"

"No. I was alone." He groaned and pressed his hands to his head again. "I'm not sure how much I drank, but I'm sure it was a lot. And then I heard something on my back porch. Or at least I thought I did. So I went outside to see."

Now Grace added some skepticism to her expression. "You'd just learned someone had murdered your fiancée, and you weren't concerned the killer might have come to your place? Your instincts weren't to call the cops?"

"No." Brian's eyes widened, and he seemed stunned at that possibility. "It never occurred to me, but I was pretty drunk by then."

Her skepticism went up a notch, though Grace silently had to admit that being drunk didn't lead to clear thinking. "What happened next?"

"I fell off the porch," he readily admitted. He pointed toward the gash on his head. "That's when I got this. Man, it started bleeding, and the blood got in my eyes. I couldn't see so I was staggering around, trying to find my way back inside."

Livvy jotted something down on a notepad, no doubt a reminder to ask SAPD to check the back porch for any blood. Grace wanted more than that, though. She believed that she had enough to get a search warrant for Brian's place, and she'd press for one once this interview was over. But that would be much easier if she could actually arrest the man, so she continued with her questions.

"Did you call out to any of your neighbors? Or try to use your phone to ask someone for help?"

"No and no." His tone was a little sharp now, and Grace hoped his annoyance, and possible anger, paid off. Angry people sometimes vented. "It was late, and I didn't want to wake anyone. And I'd left my phone inside."

"So you staggered around," Grace continued, upping her own sharp, skeptical tone, "and then what?"

Brian seemed ready to snap out a response, but then Grace could see the man visibly making an attempt to rein in his emotions. "Like I said, I tried to get back to the porch, but I guess I went the wrong way, because this morning I woke up, and I was in the drainage ditch behind my house. I must have passed out from the cut on my head and the alcohol and fallen in there."

Grace knew that could be the truth. *Could be.* But there was a reason this man was her top suspect, and she played that particular card.

"You told the cops that you were in El Paso when your fiancée was murdered," Grace stated.

There was no panic on his face, which meant he'd already known he'd be questioned about this. Of course, he had. It would have been next to impossible for him to travel all the way from El Paso, which was an eleven-hour drive. And Brian hadn't flown since Livvy had checked airline records and the man hadn't been on any flight that would have fit the timing of his drunken account.

"Yes, that," Brian muttered, and he took a moment. "I fudged the truth about that."

"You lied," Grace snapped. And she saw that flash of temper again. His jaw muscles tightened.

"Yes," he admitted. "I love my fiancée. *Loved*," he amended, "but I needed some time away from her. I felt smothered, and I didn't think she'd understand, so I made up the work story. I told it to her and her parents, and then booked a hotel in El Paso under my name. I did a digital check-in on my phone so it would look as if I'd actually been there."

Brian hadn't mentioned the possible reason he felt

smothered—because he was seeing another woman. And since he hadn't mentioned his chat with Felicity to beg her to give him an alibi, it meant Felicity had thankfully followed Grace's instructions and hadn't told Brian about her phone call to the cops.

"Felicity Martinez," Grace said simply, and she waited.

The effect was instant. Brian groaned and squeezed his eyes shut. He didn't say anything for several moments. "I'd like a lawyer," he muttered.

And that made Grace want to groan. Of course, she had known he might play the lawyer card when cornered, but there was nothing she could have done to prevent it.

Grace and Livvy stood. "If you don't have a lawyer, one can be appointed for you," Livvy reminded him.

Brian took out his phone. "I have someone," he assured them, and then stared up at her and Livvy, clearly waiting for them to leave so he could make the call.

She and the deputy did just that. They left, and Grace hoped it wouldn't be too long before the lawyer showed up. She was betting though once that happened, the attorney would demand Brian see a doctor. Which meant it would give them plenty of time to come up with a story that wouldn't paint Brian as a killer.

There was no law against being a lying, cheating scumbag, so Brian would no doubt own up to that and hope it was enough to keep his sorry butt from being arrested.

"I want you to try to get a search warrant for Brian's place," Grace whispered to Livvy the moment they were in the hall.

"I'll get right on that," Livvy assured her, and she headed in the direction of the bullpen just as Dutton came out of the observation area.

"You believe him?" Dutton immediately asked her.

Grace had to shrug because she wasn't sure. That's why she needed the warrant. Before she could fill in Dutton on that, though, she saw Rory making his way toward them. He was carrying a tablet, and judging from the look on his face, he had something important to tell them.

Or rather, show them.

"This is the artist's rendering of the man who posed as an electrician and possibly stole the knife," Rory explained.

Grace hoped it was a close enough resemblance to Brian. However, when Rory turned the tablet toward her, she didn't see any features matching their top suspect. The person was wearing what appeared to be a fake beard, just as Jamie had said, but the face was all wrong to belong to Brian.

"Is that…?" Dutton muttered, staring at the sketch.

Dutton didn't finish. Didn't need to, because Grace had seen the same thing. The sketch bore an uncanny resemblance to someone they knew.

County Sheriff Wilson Finney.

Chapter Eight

Dutton saw the dread take over Grace's expression. And he totally understood it. That sketch artist's image meant she had to question a fellow cop. A cop who already loathed her.

It was understandable why neither Jamie nor Diane had recognized Wilson. By the time Jamie had moved to the ranch, Wilson had left town to become county sheriff. As for Diane, she had moved to Renegade Canyon only two years earlier, so it was likely her and Wilson's paths had never crossed.

Grace sighed but didn't waste any time taking out her phone to call the county sheriff's office, and she put it on speaker. Moments later, a cop who identified himself as Deputy Mendoza answered.

"Sheriff Granger calling for Sheriff Finney," she said.

"He's not here. In fact, he's on his way to see you. He said he…" The deputy stopped and muttered an apology. "That he wanted to light a fire under you so you'd work harder to find Elaine's killer."

That erased some of the dread on Grace's face, and Dutton saw the flicker of anger.

"Sorry," the deputy continued. "But those were his exact words. Look, I know you and Sheriff Finney have a bad history, but that won't stop you from finding this SOB, will it?"

"It won't," Grace assured him.

"Good, because we're all ripped apart by what happened to her. She didn't deserve that. No one does."

"I agree," Grace replied. "Any idea when Sheriff Finney will be here?"

"Should be soon. He left here well over an hour ago."

That was more than enough time for the county sheriff to have made the trip, and Dutton had to hope the man wasn't setting in motion another murder or attack along the way.

Grace thanked Deputy Mendoza, ended the call and then turned to Rory. "I'll interview Sheriff Finney in my office. The location won't lessen any of his anger when he realizes why I want to talk to him, but I don't want to treat this like an official interview until I see how he reacts to the sketch. I'll also need to find out if he has an alibi for that visit to the McClennan ranch. For that, I'll need to narrow down the time that fake electrician showed up."

"Jamie is still here so I can ask her about that," Rory volunteered.

"Good," Grace muttered. "Move Jamie to the break room. I don't want her in the bullpen when Sheriff Finney arrives."

Hell. That hadn't even occurred to Dutton, that Jamie could possibly be at risk for witnessing the "electrician's" visit.

"I can arrange protective custody for her," Grace said, clearly picking up on Dutton's concern.

"Do that," Dutton insisted. He didn't want to take any chances with her safety. Then, he looked at Rory. "Ask Diane, too, about the timing of that visit," Dutton instructed him. "And the ranch hands. One of them might be able to help you pinpoint the exact time."

If several of the hands or the house staff could verify

Jamie's account, then that would help Grace narrow down whether or not Wilson could have done this.

Grace nodded her thanks for his suggestion and shifted back to Rory. "In the meantime, Livvy is working on securing a warrant for Brian's house. I also want his clothes bagged for processing and for him to be examined by a doctor or an EMT. I don't want him to use any possible injuries to get out of anything he's already said in a statement."

Rory muttered an agreement and handed her the tablet. "After I get Jamie into the break room, I'll go in and tell Brian that. He's waiting on a lawyer?"

"Yes," she confirmed. "And Brian might insist on not being examined until he talks to his lawyer. That's fine as long as he's given medical clearance before any more questions."

That was a cover-your-butt sort of move for Grace, but Dutton was glad she was taking it. Yes, the image of the fake electrician might resemble Wilson, but Brian still had to be her number-one suspect. Then again, Wilson and Brian could be working together.

But why?

Dutton could understand Brian's motive. He could have wanted Elaine out of the way so he could pursue a relationship with Felicity. The man might have felt it was the better path for him rather than merely breaking up with her. However, what was Wilson's motive?

"Do they know each other?" Dutton asked. "Wilson and Brian? I mean, Brian's fiancée did work for Wilson, so it's possible they've met."

"I'm not sure," Grace answered. She motioned for Dutton to follow her to her office while Rory went into the interview room, where she'd left Brian. "So let me try to find that out before Wilson arrives."

They went into her office, and while Grace didn't shut the door, she partially closed it, then she sank down into her chair. He saw what he already knew. The toll this was taking on her. She looked exhausted and stressed. Definitely not good.

Cursing under his breath, Dutton went to the fridge in the corner to get her a bottle of water. What he found instead were little cartons of milk.

"This doesn't seem like comfort food," he said, setting a box in front of her. "But consider it a substitute for a shot of single malt. Or in your case, a glass of wine, since that's the only thing I've ever seen you drink."

She didn't smile at his attempt to keep things light. But she did thank him and drank the milk as if chugging some much-needed wine. Dutton considered it somewhat of a miracle that it seemed to steady her. Or maybe Grace was so deep in cop mode now that she was pulling from a deep well of mental reserves. Either way, she opened her laptop and started typing.

"I'm searching for any connection between Brian and Wilson," Grace told him.

Dutton took out his phone, sent a text to the PI to check for the same thing and then began his own searches on Google and social media.

"Well, I'm not seeing anything obvious in the thumbnails of their backgrounds," she said after a couple of minutes. "Brian was born in San Antonio, and Wilson was born here. Wilson is thirty-six. Brian, twenty-seven. Brian went to college. Wilson didn't. Let me go deeper…." Her voice trailed off. "Wilson is engaged to a rookie cop at SAPD, Bailey Hannon. Now she might have a connection to Brian since they live just a couple of streets from each other."

"Check Facebook," Dutton said, turning his phone

screen so Grace could see it. "That's Elaine's page, and she posted this picture eighteen months ago when she became a deputy."

He watched as Grace studied the photo of the young deputy with her boss, Wilson, on one side of her, and Brian on the other. It was clearly a posed shot and in no way proved that the men had teamed up to kill, but they did know each other. That was a start.

"Any other photos?" she asked, and he saw her start her own social-media search.

"Maybe. This is the one that came up in the results because Elaine had tagged both Wilson and Brian." He added Bailey Hannon's name to the mix to see if there were any connections.

There was a tap at the door, and a moment later, Livvy stuck her head in. "Fastest warrant ever," Livvy said. "I sent a request to the judge, listing all the circumstantial evidence we have against Brian, and he immediately issued the warrant. SAPD will send someone out to go through Brian's house and yard," Livvy added after Grace responded with a sound of approval.

"Make sure Officer Bailey Hannon's not on the search team," Grace insisted, earning her a raised eyebrow from Livvy. "She's Wilson's fiancée."

"Ah," Livvy said. "I'll work that out with SAPD. Discreetly work it out," she added. "I'm guessing you don't want to send up a red flag about Wilson."

"You're right. So maybe just phrase the request as experienced officers to conduct the search. And that's not unreasonable. If Brian is the killer, then he might have all kinds of evidence hidden away at his place."

Livvy nodded and headed back to the bullpen, no doubt to get started on Grace's request. Grace didn't continue her computer search, though. She just sat there a moment as if processing all of this.

"If Brian's the killer, he's probably removed anything we could use against him," she said. "Well, unless he had so much faith in Felicity that he thought she'd never turn on him."

Dutton shrugged. "He did seem shocked when you brought up her name. And he did ask her to lie for him about his alibi. Not sure if that's faith or stupidity."

"Yes," Grace muttered, and she took out her phone. "I need to have another conversation with Felicity. It's possible Brian said something else to her that would help add to the circumstantial evidence."

However, before Grace could make that call, her phone dinged with a text. "It's from Rory," she said to him. "It's the time and date Jamie gave him for the visit from the fake electrician."

Good. That was a start. "I could call some of the hands to ask them. It'd take some of the workload off Rory and the rest of you."

She didn't exactly jump at the offer. Probably because he was already involved more than she wanted. But she finally nodded and said thanks under her breath. However, Dutton didn't get a chance to get started on those calls because there was a knock at the door. Rory opened it, but he didn't manage to say anything before their visitor stormed in.

Wilson.

Dutton wasn't the least bit surprised to see that Wilson was already past the stage of being merely angry. There was rage in the hardened muscles on the man's face.

"You've got Elaine's fiancé in custody for her murder, and you didn't bother to tell me?" Wilson demanded. "I always knew you were incompetent. And your word means nothing. You said you'd keep me in the loop on this investigation, and then you go behind my back."

Dutton got to his feet and had to rein in his own temper. He wanted to dole out some venom of his own, but that would only escalate an already tense situation. Wilson had obviously come in here gunning for a fight, and that anger was going to soar once he realized what Grace was about to show him.

In contrast, Grace stayed seated, and she looked way calmer than Dutton could have ever managed to appear. He figured it was a facade, that she was fuming inside, but she was clearly holding it together.

"How did you know Brian Waterman was here?" she asked.

Wilson seemed ready to spew out his response, but he hesitated. "Cassie."

Dutton hadn't expected that, and obviously neither had Grace. "How did Cassie know he was here, and why did she call you about it?"

Again, he hesitated, but there was still enough anger brewing inside him that he snapped out a response. "She was at the diner when she saw a man with blood on his shirt come in here. She asked around, and someone told her it was Brian."

Grace glanced at Rory, who was still in the doorway behind Wilson, and the look she gave him had Rory stepping away, no doubt to find out who'd given that info to Cassie. It wasn't a secret, but no one should be blabbing about it, either.

"I don't have Brian Waterman in custody," she stated to Wilson, her still calm voice matching her expression. "He came in voluntarily and is waiting on his lawyer so I can continue to interview him. He lied about his alibi."

She didn't add the whole story about Felicity, and Dutton wondered if she would. Maybe she'd wait until she had ruled out Wilson as a suspect. If she could rule him out, that is.

"Why did he have blood on him?" Wilson snarled.

"He said he got drunk and fell." She never took her eyes off Wilson, so she was obviously watching to see the man's reaction. And she got a reaction alright.

"Is he lying?" Wilson demanded. "Was it Elaine's blood?"

"I'm not sure. We've taken a sample, and it's at the lab."

Wilson huffed. "You should be pressing to get those results ASAP," he stormed. "You should be on the phone with the lab right now, demanding—"

She stopped him by holding up the tablet. At first, Wilson just looked confused, and then he went in for a closer look. Dutton moved, too, putting himself at an angle so he could see Wilson's face. There didn't seem to be any shock, though the man might just be good at concealing his emotions. He was a cop, after all.

"What is that?" Wilson asked.

"A sketch of a man wearing a disguise who lied his way into the main house at the McClennan ranch," Grace answered, and then she waited.

Wilson studied it some more. "What did he do?"

"He likely stole the knife and used it to murder Elaine," Grace explained.

That caused Wilson to stare at the screen several moments longer. And then he cursed. When his gaze went back to Grace, there was a new wave of fury in his eyes. "You think that's me."

"It looks like you," Dutton volunteered, earning him a glare.

Wilson exploded with profanities and went on for several seconds. "This proves you're lousy at your job, Sheriff Granger." He tapped his badge. "I'm a cop, not a killer."

Again, Grace managed to look unfazed by that. "Is that you in the sketch?" she asked. "And would you be willing to stand in a lineup so I can eliminate you as a suspect?"

If looks could have killed, Grace would have been dead. "No and no," Wilson stated through clenched teeth. "It's not me and I won't be in a lineup that you've arranged to try to set me up." He put his hands on his hips and his glare turned mocking. "You're really scraping the bottom of the barrel with this theory. I didn't know you could be so petty."

"I need to eliminate you as a suspect," Grace returned, sounding not petty but like the solid cop she was.

"This eliminates me." Wilson tapped his badge again and started pacing. Not that he could go far in the small office, but he attempted it, all the while continuing to mutter profanities.

Grace jotted down a time and date on a note and slid it across the desk for Wilson to see. Dutton could see it was the info Jamie had given them. "I also need to know if you have an alibi for then."

That definitely didn't improve Wilson's mood, but he whipped out his phone as if he'd declared war. He opened an app and scrolled through it. "I was at work that day. If you don't believe me, you can call my dispatcher and ask for the duty rosters."

"Did you leave work at any time?" Grace pressed.

Wilson attempted an answer, but his anger got the best of him, and he had to take a moment to settle. "Probably. That was two months ago, so I can't say for certain, but I normally go out for lunch." He stopped and surprised Dutton by not cursing, but sighing. "I didn't kill two cops," he insisted. "And I didn't put on a fake beard and steal a knife."

Grace didn't say anything. She just sat there, waiting, with her eyes drilling into Wilson.

The man sighed again. "I'm going to give you some leeway here because you're pregnant and hormonal," Wilson said.

Again, Grace didn't respond with venom. Though that's what Dutton wanted to do. He suspected she did, too, but Grace merely sat and waited for Wilson to continue.

"I'm going to give you leeway," he repeated. "Because we're all on edge about these murders. Hell, my fiancée is a cop. I'm scared for her. Scared that the next time I kiss her goodbye before work, that'll be the last time I see her. And then I come in here and you show me that." He flung his index finger at the tablet. "It's disgusting you think I could do any of this."

"Yet I had to ask because this is part of the job," Grace reminded him. She didn't add more. Again, she just waited, and she didn't have to wait long before Wilson pointed to the sketch again.

"The real killer wants you to think that's me so you'll go on a wild-goose chase and waste time. Time he or she will use to kill again. *She*," he said with emphasis, staring at Grace.

For a moment, Dutton thought Wilson was about to accuse Grace of being the killer, but then he added something that had Dutton's stomach twisting.

"Is Cassie a suspect?" Wilson pressed.

Grace didn't alter her expression one bit. "Why do you ask that?"

"Because she sure as hell should be." Wilson shifted his attention to Dutton now. "Hell hath no fury like a woman scorned."

"So you're saying because Cassie is upset with our

breakup that she's gone on a killing spree?" Dutton countered. Though that very idea had occurred to him, especially since Ike had admitted that Cassie could have stolen the knife.

Wilson hesitated. Then he huffed. "I'm just saying that I hope Sheriff Granger is looking at this from all angles. That's what good cops do."

"Which is why she wanted to question you about the sketch," Dutton quickly pointed out.

Oh, Wilson didn't care for that, but he seemed to put a choke hold on spouting out any more profanities. "I like Cassie," Wilson said. "I think she's probably not the killer, but she has motive in spades. And I don't want that motive spilling over to my fiancée just so a scorned woman can cover her tracks."

"I don't want that, either," Grace assured him, and now she stood. "Trust me when I say the stakes are the highest for Dutton and me. It isn't just our lives at risk, but also our child's. I'll investigate anyone who might be the killer or anyone helping them."

Wilson stared at her a long time as if looking for a way to punch holes in what she'd just said. He didn't try that, though. "Call me the second you get lab results back on that blood you took from Elaine's fiancé," he demanded. And with that, he turned and walked out, slamming the door behind him.

Grace stood there a moment before she blew out a long breath. Dutton saw the tremble in her hand then, but didn't go to her. Though that's exactly what he wanted to do.

"So much anger in him," she muttered. "And, yes, I believe he's capable of murder because he hates the two of us that much."

Dutton wished he could disagree with that, but he

couldn't. As far as he was concerned, Wilson, Cassie and Brian were all suspects.

Grace winced a little and slid her hand over her stomach. "The baby kicked during that entire conversation."

"And yet you didn't show any signs of it," Dutton remarked, watching her hand move over their baby. "No sign of hormones and pregnancy," he joked, repeating Wilson's childish insult.

One corner of her mouth lifted, just as he'd hoped it would. Dutton wanted to lighten this moment for her and wished he could take all of her stress onto his own shoulders.

Grace reached out, took his hand and placed it on her stomach. It felt odd to touch her, especially since they'd spent the last five months making sure there was no physical contact between them. But there was contact now, not just with Grace and him. Dutton also felt the slight thumps of the baby.

His breath went thin, and he got a surge of...well, he wasn't sure, but it felt good. For something so small, it certainly packed a punch, and in that moment, Dutton understood why parents gushed about their kids.

He looked at Grace and saw that she was smiling. He got that. She was able to feel these little miracle kicks even when dealing with a pain like Wilson. Even when things seemed so dangerous and uncertain.

His gaze automatically dropped to her mouth, and Dutton had to fight the overwhelming urge to kiss her. It was an urge he might not have been able to suppress had her phone not rang.

Grace sighed but then also seemed a little relieved. He got that. A kiss would feel amazing, but it would skyrocket the uncertainty and maybe cause them to lose focus.

She took out her phone and glanced at the screen before she answered it. "It's Larry Crandall," she said.

He was the head CSI who'd been working the crime scenes by the ranch, so Dutton was very much interested in this call. Thankfully, Grace put it on speaker.

"Sheriff Granger, this is Larry," the CSI greeted her. "We found something."

Chapter Nine

Grace realized she was holding her breath. And hoping. Because she really wanted the CSI to tell her that they'd just gotten a huge break in the investigation and could now find the killer.

"What did you find?" Grace asked.

"Fibers caught on a splinter in the fence post. They haven't been here long and don't match the rope or anything the victim was wearing," Larry said. "It's possible it's from the killer or maybe the carpet or floor mats in the killer's vehicle. They're gray," he added.

Grace's mind began to whirl with possibilities. She didn't need a search warrant to glance through the windows of the suspects' vehicles and see the color of the carpet.

"Obviously, I'll get these to the lab right away," Larry assured her. "And while I've got you on the phone, the team out at your house found some tire tracks in the mud on the trail behind your house."

She knew which one he meant. It was only about twenty yards away and was hidden in some trees. But Grace had to mentally shake her head.

"The stabbed woman came from the front of the house," Grace said.

"Yes, and there are no unusual tracks there. Just the ones from the cruisers. I guess it's possible the killer dropped her off toward the front of your house and then parked on the trail."

That made sense, but it also meant the woman's blood would likely be in the vehicle the killer was driving.

Grace thanked Larry for the info, and the moment she hung up, she fired off a text to Eden to ask her to have Brian's car impounded and examined. That was the easiest of the three since it was in the parking lot. Checking the carpet in Cassie's vehicle wouldn't be that hard, either. Wilson's, though, would be tricky.

"You want me to have my PI check and see if any of our suspects rented a vehicle?" Dutton asked.

She nearly smiled but didn't repeat her comment about him sounding like a cop. Because she was stretching her deputies thin, she nearly took him up on his offer, but she had a different task in mind.

"Could your PI go to the county sheriff's office and take a discreet look at the carpet inside Wilson's vehicle?" she asked. "And maybe a glance inside the other cruisers as well? Discreet," she repeated. "Nothing illegal. If I send a deputy, someone there might recognize them and report back to Wilson."

"Let sleeping dogs lie," he muttered while he composed a text, no doubt to his PI. "Or maybe this is more like not poking a rattlesnake with a short stick."

Grace nodded. "If Wilson is the killer, then enraging him might provoke him into committing another murder. He has a very short fuse, and I'd rather not set it off."

Dutton gave his own nod and was finishing up the text when there was a knock at the door. A moment later, Rory came in.

"Just wanted you to know that the EMTs are here with Brian," Rory said. "He didn't refuse the exam."

"Good. And the lawyer?" she asked.

"Not here yet, but I did just call the hospital to see if there was any change in Georgia's condition. She had to go in for a second round of surgery for internal bleeding."

That definitely didn't sound good. "And there's still nothing to connect Georgia with Renegade Canyon, the other two victims, Dutton or me?"

"Nothing. But her sister is at the hospital, and I was about to head there to have a chat with her."

"Good idea." Because it was possible the sister might know something that hadn't turned up in any searches.

Rory stepped back, but then had to stop from bumping into Cassie, who'd come up behind him. Grace was thankful she hadn't had to jump through hoops to get Cassie in for questioning, but it took Grace a couple of seconds to mentally switch gears. And to steel herself for what would possibly turn into an ugly situation. She could tell from Cassie's expression that the woman was already riled.

"My PA said you called and that you wanted to see me?" Cassie said, the words sounding like an accusation. She spared Dutton a glance and then huffed as if to say "of course, you're still here with Grace."

"Yes, I need to ask you some questions about a visit you paid to Ike two months ago," Grace explained.

"A visit…" Cassie's words trailed off, and her eyes widened. "Why would Ike tell you about that?"

Dutton stood. "I'll be in the break room," he muttered.

Cassie huffed again and folded her arms over her chest. "Wait." She moved in front of Dutton. "Did you put your father up to this, whatever *this* is?"

Dutton looked her straight in the eyes. "I don't put Ike up to anything," he told Cassie. There was just a smidge of cockiness in that statement.

Cassie's attention flew back to Grace, and for a moment it seemed as if she was about to accuse her of the same thing, but then she must have remembered that Ike would never be swayed by anything Grace said. Just the opposite.

"So what is this?" Cassie demanded, and once again, she moved in front of Dutton to stop him from leaving.

Dutton huffed and glanced at Grace to get her take on this. She motioned for him to stay put. Technically, this wasn't an official interview and couldn't be. Not without something with more "teeth" than Ike's account. So Grace just went ahead and laid it out there for Cassie.

"Ike told me that you'd visited the ranch two months ago and that means you had the opportunity to take a knife that went missing."

Cassie seemed to do some kind of mental double take, making Grace wonder what the woman had thought this meeting was about. Had Cassie thought she was going to be questioned about something else?

If so, what?

The woman quickly regrouped, though, and the anger came back into her eyes. "No, I didn't steal a knife and then use it to murder a woman I never met. I'm not a psychopathic killer. I'm a respected businesswoman who shouldn't be treated like a criminal."

Grace didn't point out that this wasn't criminal treatment. If it was, she would have Mirandized Cassie and had this chat on the record in an interview room, probably with the woman's lawyer present.

"I was merely asking," Grace replied instead. "I have to either verify or eliminate any and all possible evidence, and sometimes I have to do that by asking hard questions."

"Well, you should have known the answer because you know I'm not capable of something like that." Cassie gave a dry laugh. "And if I were going to kill someone, why in the name of heaven would I have used Ike's knife to do it? That makes no sense."

"It does if you wanted to get back at me," Dutton pointed out.

Cassie gave him a withering look. "You no longer mean enough to me for me to do that. If I wanted to get back at you, I'd pressure the town council for that recall vote to get Grace out of office."

She stopped again, shifting her attention to Grace, and in that stare Grace saw that was indeed Cassie's intention. Pressure just might work, too. But she couldn't think about that now. The murder investigation had to be her focus.

"Is that all, Sheriff?" Cassie snarled.

Grace didn't respond but instead sent a quick text to Rory to make sure he'd gotten a look at the carpeting in Cassie's car. Rory was equally quick with his reply.

I did, Rory texted. It's gray.

Grace looked at Cassie again. "Would you be willing to let us examine your car?" she asked, purposely not mentioning the carpet.

Cassie looked as if Grace had just asked her for her first-born, and the woman aimed a look at Dutton that seemed a mix of both outrage and confusion. "I know we aren't together any longer, but I can't believe you'd stand there and let her treat me like this."

"She's doing her job," Dutton said.

"Well, she can do it without snooping in my car when she has no right." Judging from the increasing volume of Cassie's voice, Grace thought the woman's tirade would just continue.

It didn't.

Cassie stopped, then shifted back to Grace. "Are you

doing this because of what the CSIs found at the crime scene?"

Grace tried very hard not to blink. It was poker-face time. "What do you mean?"

Cassie huffed. "I heard that the CSIs are back at the fence."

So maybe Cassie was fishing, but Grace wasn't playing. "A CSI will often examine the scene several times. It's routine."

"No," Cassie argued. "This wasn't routine."

Grace merely lifted an eyebrow, an invitation for Cassie to continue.

Once again, Cassie huffed. "A friend was driving by and saw the CSIs and stopped. She said they looked excited, and that one of them made a call. That doesn't sound routine."

Grace considered the possibility that the "friend" was actually Cassie. But there was nothing criminal about observing CSIs unless the person actually trespassed or went onto the crime scene. If that had happened, Larry would have let her know.

"Anything found at the scene will be processed and evaluated," Grace finally said. "And I can't discuss the details of an active investigation with you."

Oh, that statement didn't please Cassie. She aimed a glare at Dutton. "But you've discussed it with him."

Grace didn't mention that Dutton was a potential target and not a suspect, and thankfully her silence let Cassie fill in the blanks. "You'll regret this," Cassie warned them and then stormed out.

Well, that was two people she'd managed to rile in the past hour. Three, if she counted Brian. And while this was part of the job, Grace felt at the moment that being sheriff was taking a serious toll on her. Dutton must have seen that on her face, because on a sigh, he shut the door and went to her.

And pulled her into his arms.

Grace nearly went with the knee-jerk reaction of pushing him away. But she didn't. It was ironic, but Dutton was the one person who truly knew the fear she felt over the baby being in danger. That shared camaraderie, though, was a dangerous thing.

Still, she didn't move away.

Didn't stop him from easing her closer to him until they were body-to-body. Breath-to-breath. She purposely didn't look up at him. No way could she resist him if she did that. So she just stood there and took everything he was giving her. And he was giving her plenty. Not just comfort, but that swirl of heat that seemed to make her forget the urgency of their current situation.

"I can't do this," she muttered, but still didn't move away.

He did, though. Despite his bad-boy reputation, Grace knew a statement like that from her was as good as a no. "I, uh, just hate to see you like this," he said.

"I hate to be like this," she confirmed. Now she risked looking at him and saw the traces of heat still in his eyes. "Mercy," she muttered. "I wish I could take a pill or a vaccine to stop this heat."

Dutton smiled, that damnable smile that made him look so hot. "Trust me, I've wished the same thing about you." Then, he lifted his shoulder in a shrug. "Well, I did before I got you pregnant, and after that, well, let's just say I need a pill to stop spinning certain fantasies."

Grace felt what she thought might be a shiver of fear, excitement and worry all rolled into one. Dutton hadn't meant *that*. Had he? He must be talking about sex and not some fantasy about them riding off into the sunset together with their baby. For once, she hoped it was the sex. The attraction was a lot easier to deal with than a lifetime commitment with the one man who could shake the very core of her world.

Thankfully, Grace didn't have to respond because Dutton's phone rang, and when he looked at the screen, he muttered, "It's the PI."

"Jake, you're on speaker," Dutton told the man. "And Sheriff Grace Granger is listening."

"Good," the PI said, "because she'll want to hear this. Eleven years ago, Grace's mother arrested two teenagers. Delaney Moreland and Keith Cassaine. They were sixteen."

Grace didn't have to press her memory to recall the names despite it being over a decade ago. "Underage drinking. Delaney choked on her own vomit in the back seat of the cruiser while my mother was bringing them in."

"Bingo," Jake confirmed. "And you were one of the deputies who assisted in the arrest. Delaney's parents filed a lawsuit against your mother and the entire police department, but they lost."

"Yes, because the ME stated that Delaney likely would have died from alcohol poisoning if she hadn't choked."

Still, that hadn't lessened the guilt her mother and she had felt. A girl had died, and they hadn't been able to prevent that.

"Do you think this is connected to the murders of two cops?" Grace asked.

"A strong possibility, because shortly after Delaney's death, Keith Cassaine changed his name." The PI paused a heartbeat. "These days, he goes by Brian Waterman."

Chapter Ten

Dutton forwarded Grace the email of the report that Jake had just sent him, and then he moved a chair next to hers so they could read the arrest report on Keith Cassaine, aka Brian Waterman.

The man who was probably now at the top of Grace's suspect list.

He'd never read an actual police report and saw that it was broken into four sections. The first contained the names and photos of those involved, the date and the arresting officer, Sheriff Aileen Granger. Below that were sections labeled Details of the Event, Actions Taken and Summary. Grace skipped to the summary that her mother had written eleven years ago.

On her way home from work around ten on a Friday night, Aileen had witnessed a car driving erratically, so she'd pulled it over. Brian had been driving and Delaney was the passenger. There was an open bottle of tequila on the console, and both teens were visibly intoxicated. They both failed breathalyzers. Aileen had called for backup, and when Grace had arrived, they'd taken the pair into custody, putting them in the back of Aileen's cruiser.

On that fateful night, Grace had followed Aileen in her own vehicle to the police station, but along the way, Aileen had stopped to try to resuscitate Delaney. Grace had been the one to call the ambulance, but by the time it arrived, Delaney was already dead.

Maybe out of shock and grief and fueled by the alcohol, Brian had become violent and had attempted to assault Aileen. He'd failed, though, because Grace had managed to restrain him. After they'd returned to the police station, it'd been Grace who'd actually arrested him because Aileen had likely been dealing with the aftermath of Delaney's death.

"I need to talk to my mother about this," Grace said. "Give her a heads-up that this old case could be linked to the current murders." She paused. "She'll realize right away that she could be the motive for the killer and that she could also be the actual target."

Yeah, Aileen would understand that. "Any chance your mother will let you put her in protective custody?"

"None," Grace quickly responded, and she sent a text to her mother to give her the basics. "This is better than a phone call since she won't want to discuss it until she's had a chance to refresh her memory."

That didn't surprise him about not nixing the protective custody. In fact, it would likely feel like an insult to the woman who'd been a sheriff for three decades.

"There's a separate report on Delaney," Grace continued once she finished the text. She pulled up that report as well and put it side by side with the one they'd been reading.

It was all there. More details of Aileen's attempts to revive the teenager, along with toxicology reports. Delaney's blood alcohol content, BLC, had been 0.40 percent. Since anything higher than 0.08 would be legally over the limit, Delaney had obviously had way too much to drink. Brian was over the limit, too, but nowhere as high as Delaney.

Dutton switched his attention to the mug shot of the then sixteen-year-old Brian. Obviously, he wasn't looking his best in the photo. He was probably still drunk and in shock, and he was well past the disheveled stage. What stood out about him was his mop of ginger hair. It fell in shaggy chunks all around his acne-scarred face.

"Brian looks nothing like he did when he was a teenager," Dutton pointed out.

Grace made a sound of agreement. "Different hair color, and he's at least fifty pounds heavier now than he was back then. He must have had some cosmetic procedure to get rid of those acne scars. And he legally changed his name when he was eighteen." She stopped, then sighed. "Still, I should have recognized him."

"Yeah, because you should have special cop powers that allow you to recall every feature of every face you've seen over the past eleven years."

Dutton added a smile and enjoyed both the roll of her eyes and that sliver of heat he saw when their gazes met. He was tired of cursing that heat. Tired of having to fight it. But even the heat couldn't override that Grace and he should keep fighting it for no other reason than to focus on the here and now. On this investigation, that might just save some lives.

"I'll question him about this when I've got him back in interview," she said, obviously moving the conversation in the right direction.

No smiles now. Minimal heat as well. And she kept the focus on the job as she downloaded the report from the PI. Still sitting side by side, they read it together, but they'd barely gotten started before Grace got a text.

"It's from Rory," she said as she continued to scan the report. "Brian's lawyer is here. I'll give them a few minutes before going in. That'll give me time to get a better picture of what Brian's been doing for the past eleven years. Wow,"

Grace said when something obviously caught her attention. "He had a second arrest a year after the one here."

Yeah, he had. And it had been for assault on his sister. So Brian had a temper and could be violent. First, the attempted attack on Aileen and then this. "But no jail time," Dutton pointed out.

"No, because he was charged as a juvenile. A surprise because of his previous conviction for what happened here. I'm guessing either he had a very lenient judge or a very good lawyer. Maybe both."

"His family comes from some money," Dutton said, referring to the man's parents' net worth, which Jake had included in the report. They were worth nearly a million. However, the same couldn't be said for Brian, who seemed to be living paycheck to paycheck.

"Yes," she muttered. "It'll be worth the time to have a quick chat with his parents to see if they've cut him off financially." She paused. "I'd better let Livvy or Eden handle that, though. They weren't deputies eleven years ago, and Brian's parents might not want to speak to anyone who'd been involved in his arrest."

Good idea, and he continued to read the PI's report while Grace texted Eden to contact the parents. Maybe they'd be able to give Eden some insight about their son. Since Brian had changed his name, it was possible there'd been a rift.

"So Keith changed his name to Brian during his first year of college," Grace stated, continuing with the report. "I'm guessing because he might have wanted a fresh start. And there are no more arrests. He got a degree in business and works for a real-estate company. SAPD has agreed to send someone to get a statement from Brian's boss. Austin PD is getting a statement from Felicity."

Dutton figured Grace must have requested that, with two

of the many texts and calls she'd made in the past twelve hours.

"And you've got Brian's vehicle," Dutton reminded her. "So if the carpet fibers are a match to those the CSIs found, then you can make an arrest this morning."

Dutton knew that was a long shot, though. So did Grace.

"I doubt it's a match or he wouldn't have driven it here and risked the possibility of it being scrutinized by cops," she said, voicing what Dutton was thinking.

If Brian was the killer, then this visit was all some kind of ploy, maybe to try to convince Grace that he was innocent. Or to continue a sick cat-and-mouse game with her.

"What are the chances you'll get warrants to search Cassie's and Wilson's vehicles?" he asked.

"Zero." She gave a weary sigh. "Everything I have against them is circumstantial, and unlike Brian, I can't even prove they've lied to me. At least a lie could be construed as obstruction of justice. Added to that, a warrant likely wouldn't produce anything, anyway."

"Because they probably wouldn't have used their own vehicles," he muttered. And he thought of something else. "I can have my PI look into rental-car records for the area. Maybe the killer used one and left some kind of paper trail."

Grace made a sound of agreement and took a moment, obviously processing that possibility. "Let me do that search through official channels, though. I don't want anything questioned or thrown out if there are any doubts about the chain of custody if this turns out to be evidence we need for a trial."

Dutton understood, but he hated that he couldn't do something to speed things along. Grace and her deputies were already stretched thin, and he was betting that neither

Cassie nor Wilson would be forthcoming to help Grace if it turned out one of them was the killer.

That brought Dutton to another question. "Would Cassie have been able to lift the two dead cops?"

Grace shrugged. "Both dead women had slight builds, and Cassie could have used the over-the-shoulder fireman's carry to get them from the vehicle to the fence. It wouldn't have been easy, but she could have managed it. Plus, she's familiar with the area and has motive."

"Yeah, motive because of me," he said under his breath.

Grace met his gaze, and for a moment he thought she was about to lecture him on not taking on that kind of blame. She didn't. She stunned him by brushing her mouth over his. Apparently, she'd stunned herself, too, because she immediately jerked away from him.

"Sorry," she blurted at the same time he insisted, "Don't you dare apologize."

Dutton didn't add more. Something like it barely qualified as a kiss, anyway. Or that maybe it'd helped relieve a little stress. It certainly had for him, anyway. But for Grace, she probably saw this as a serious lapse in concentration.

She got to her feet. "I'll go in and interview Brian now. You can watch on the video feed."

It seemed to Dutton that she couldn't get out of the office fast enough. Yep, that kiss was weighing on her. It was weighing on him, too, but in a totally different kind of way. It'd been a reminder of just how intense his need was for her.

Her phone dinged with a text, and he saw Aileen's name on the screen. "'I'm sorry the past has come back on you like this,'" Grace said, reading aloud. "'Sorry about the whole damn mess of it. And, no, I won't go into protective custody. Keep me posted about any developments and do what you need to do to get this pathetic excuse for a human off the streets.'"

Grace sighed, no doubt because her mother had indeed denied the protection. Which she just might need. In fact, it was possible that Grace and he were the decoy targets and that the person Brian wanted to punish was Aileen. That theory only worked, though, if Brian was the actual killer.

"Ready for the interview?" Grace asked Livvy when she went out into the bullpen.

Livvy immediately nodded and got up. "SAPD is at Brian's place now," Livvy explained as they walked down the hall. "Fingers crossed they find something we can use to get him to confess."

"Fingers crossed," Grace agreed in a mutter, but she didn't sound especially hopeful. Again, that was probably because this particular killer wouldn't have left something incriminating for the cops to find.

Grace made eye contact with Dutton before he went into the observation area, and he saw that the laptop was still on the table. The screen was blank, but Grace or Livvy must have activated the camera because soon he saw the feed of them in the room with Brian and a smartly dressed woman who must be his attorney. Brian was sporting a bandage on his forehead and a clean T-shirt and jogging pants.

"Sheriff Granger and Deputy Walsh resuming interview with Brian Waterman," Grace stated. "Also present is his attorney. Please state your name for the record."

"Cecily Monroe," the woman said.

Grace pinned her gaze to Brian. "You didn't mention earlier that you knew me. Why not?"

Because Dutton could see their faces, he noted that neither Brian nor his lawyer showed any surprise over the comment and question, which likely meant Brian had told the lawyer about it.

"I don't like talking about my past," Brian replied. "It was a painful time for me, and I worked hard to put it all behind me."

"But you did recognize me," Grace pressed.

"Yes. You were a deputy when my girlfriend died," he said.

Dutton listened for any venom in those words, but didn't hear any. It was possibly there, though, and Brian was managing to keep it under wraps. After all, the anger over Delaney's death could be motive.

"I was," Grace said. "Your fiancée's murder must have triggered some memories of your girlfriend's death."

Again, nothing obvious flashed on Brian's face. "It did, but like I said, I've tried to put all of that behind me."

"Is that why you changed your name and appearance?" Grace asked.

"In part," he readily admitted. "But my parents disinherited me after my arrest, and I thought it best if I didn't have any association with them. Name included, since Keith is also my father's name. As for the hair color, well, that's just a personal preference. I wasn't fond of the ginger and thought this better suited me."

Grace stared at him for several moments. *"Arrests,"* she said.

It seemed to take Brian a moment to realize she was correcting his use of the singular. "Yes, arrests." Now his voice did tighten a little. "That happened so long ago that I don't even think about it. But I suppose I should. It made me turn my life around." There was some cockiness to his tone now.

It was short-lived, though.

Because he must have recalled what had prompted him to end the earlier interview and call in a lawyer.

"You'll want to know about Felicity," Brian volunteered. He glanced at his lawyer. "I've made a full disclosure to her, and now I'll do the same for you. I had an affair with Felicity Martinez. *Had*," he repeated. "I ended things with her two weeks ago, and she was very upset. I suspect she had some not-so-pleasant things to say about me."

So Brian was trying to get ahead of this, probably by lying, since Felicity hadn't mentioned a breakup. It was possible it had happened, and maybe that would come out when she was interviewed by Austin PD.

"You broke up with the woman you were cheating with?" Grace asked.

The lawyer huffed and looked ready to object, but Brian touched her arm to silence her. "Yes, I broke up with her because I realized just how much I loved Elaine. I wanted to marry her and start a family." His voice cracked. "And now, I've lost her."

Grace gave him a moment, but Dutton figured she was thinking this could all be an act. He wished suspects were equipped with a built-in lie detector that would go off during questioning.

He stopped, replayed that notion and nearly smiled. Yeah, sometimes he did think like a cop.

"Is it true that Elaine was on the verge of breaking up with you?" Grace asked. And she asked it with a straight face, too. Dutton knew it was a bluff, that she hadn't gotten even a whiff of that so far in the investigation.

Brian's eyes widened. "No. What? No," he repeated and was visibly flustered. "Did Felicity tell you that, because if so, it's a lie."

"That didn't come from Felicity," Grace assured him, maybe so Brian wouldn't take aim at his former lover.

"Then, who?" Brian demanded. Now it was his lawyer who touched his arm as if to settle and silence him.

Grace fixed her hard stare on Brian. "I'm not at liberty to divulge that."

Oh, that didn't please the man, and Brian looked on the verge of a verbal explosion before he seemed to rein it all in.

"Well, whoever told you lied," Brian concluded. "Or maybe you're the liar. Cops can do that. They can lie through their teeth and try to entrap innocent people." He rammed his thumb against his chest. "I'm innocent, and I won't be railroaded by some cop who clearly doesn't have a clue how to investigate my fiancée's murder."

Grace didn't appear fazed by the insult. "Shortly after Delaney's death, you made threats against the Renegade Canyon Police Department."

Dutton didn't know that for sure, but it was a good guess on Grace's part. Brian had been a hotheaded teenager and had probably done some threatening. Maybe even on social media. And since that might be an avenue to explore, Dutton sent another text to Jake so he could add the search to his to-do list. He also told the PI to employ as many other investigators as needed to get the job done quickly.

"I was upset," Brian responded after a whispered conversation with his lawyer. "So I possibly said some things I shouldn't have."

"You made threats," Grace repeated. "You attempted to assault the sheriff during the lawful arrest she made on you. Obviously, you have quite a temper, so I have to wonder if that temper ignited when Elaine wanted to end the engagement."

There. Dutton saw it in Brian's expression. The anger,

yes, but there was something more. Maybe the truth. And in that moment, Dutton realized this was a man who could kill.

But had Brian done that?

It was possible, but he could say the same thing about Cassie or Wilson. And both of them had motive to include Dutton in the death threat. Brian didn't. As far as Dutton knew, he'd never crossed paths with the man. He made a mental note to check that. It was possible they'd had an encounter that he didn't recall.

He was about to do a Google search with both Brian's name and his own when his phone rang, and he saw Jamie's name on the screen. Dutton instantly got a bad feeling, since the girl rarely called him.

"Anything wrong?" Dutton asked the moment he answered.

"Yes," the girl said, and her voice was filled with fear. "Uncle Ike brought me home to get my backpack before he dropped me off at school. He was waiting in his truck. But when I came back out, he wasn't there."

Even though there could be a reasonable explanation for this, Dutton's stomach stayed in a hard knot. "Maybe he went inside, too. Did you look for him?"

"Yes, I looked," Jamie insisted, her words coming out quickly. "And he didn't come in. The alarm is set to chime when a door opens, and I would have heard it. I didn't." A sob tore from her throat. "Dutton, his truck door is open, and there's blood on the seat."

Chapter Eleven

Grace tried not to do a mental worst-case scenario as she and Dutton drove to the McClennan ranch. Hard not to think the worst, though, when there was a killer on the loose.

A killer she thought she might have in an interview room.

But if this was an attack, then Brian couldn't have possibly done it, since she'd been grilling him with questions at the time of Jamie's call. Still, it was possible the man had an accomplice or had hired someone to do this.

Whatever this was.

Jamie had said there was blood, but Grace was hoping that maybe Ike had somehow injured himself and had left his vehicle to get help. Though that didn't explain why he wouldn't have stayed put and called for help. Or simply gone inside, where Jamie would have seen and heard him.

"Keep looking," Dutton told his head ranch hand that he'd called as Grace and he had been hurrying out of the police station.

Hurrying with caution… After all, this could be some kind of ploy by the killer to lure them out, so that's why they were in the bullet-resistant cruiser with Rory and Livvy in another cruiser directly behind them.

"Nearly all the ranch hands are searching for Ike," Dutton said to her the moment he finished the call. "The house staff and two other hands are inside the house with Jamie, in case...well, just in case."

Apparently, he didn't want to spell out the worst, either, and Grace was glad Dutton had been so quick to organize a search for his father and an immediate fix to protect Jamie. It sickened her to think the girl could be in danger.

Because if the killer had taken Ike, or if a hired gun had done that, then he or she could still be at the ranch, ready to attack. Grace didn't want Jamie caught in the middle of a gunfight.

During her frantic call with Dutton, Jamie had mentioned that there'd been a big truck by the bunkhouse, and while she hadn't known exactly why it was there, Dutton had been able to provide that info. It'd been a scheduled delivery of some new equipment for the stables. Dutton had vetted the driver, the helper he'd brought with him and the company itself. However, that didn't mean someone hadn't snuck into the truck and then onto the ranch.

"You're sure Jamie didn't see anyone lurking around when she went inside for the backpack?" Grace asked Dutton.

As expected, he shook his head, and Grace knew he had indeed asked the girl that specific question. Jamie hadn't seen anyone or anything unusual. Dutton hadn't pressed her, probably because he'd wanted to get off the line and contact the ranch hands. But it was something Grace would need to question her about.

"I'll call her back now that we're on the way," Dutton muttered.

"Hold off on that," Grace said. "It's a long shot, a bad one, but I don't want anyone to use the sound of her phone ringing to pinpoint her location in the house. You told her to keep away from the windows and to lock herself in her bedroom with her nanny, the cook and one of the house-keepers. And she reactivated the security system. That's the best we can do for right now."

Also, Jamie would no doubt call them if she did hear anyone, or if someone tried to break into the house. For that to happen, the intruder would apparently have to get past several ranch hands. With a house that size, it was possible for someone to do that, but then the alarm would go off to let those inside know what was going on.

"Maybe Eden will see something on the security cam-era feed," Dutton muttered.

Yes, maybe. Dutton had given Eden the access codes to the feed, so she could study it while they were at the ranch. Even though she figured the cameras were top-notch, that didn't mean someone hadn't managed to evade them. They hoped, though, there hadn't been any evasion and that the person had been captured in the footage.

"I won't suggest you staying in the cruiser while the hands finish checking for a gunman," Dutton said. "But just know, that's what I wish you could do. Hell, I wish I could wrap you in bulletproof bubble wrap instead of just that Kevlar vest."

Yes, she was wearing a vest. All of them were, except Dutton, who'd turned down the offer since his ranch hands wouldn't have that particular safety measure. And while Grace appreciated his concern about her, he was right. She had to do her job, and right now, the job was finding his father and maybe catching a killer in the process. Even if this was a hired gun, if they managed to catch the person, then that might lead them straight to the killer.

Even though it took less than ten minutes to get to the ranch, it felt like an eternity before Grace took the final turn to get there. Of course, she had to pass the fence line along the way, the very part where two bodies had been left. She automatically checked, just to make sure there wasn't another one. But no one was there. Even the CSIs had apparently already left.

They passed the pastures, where horses were grazing by a shady pond. It seemed like much too serene of a scene, considering what might be happening at the ranch. She imagined the frantic search that had to be going on. And she was right. The moment she drove through the wrought-iron gates, she saw several ranch hands hurrying between two of the massive barns on the grounds. There were two smaller barns and another outbuilding.

Plenty of places for a killer to be lying in wait.

She stopped the cruiser right at the porch steps and turned to Dutton. "I need to go in and talk to Jamie and the house-keeper," she explained. "They might have seen something."

He nodded and used his phone to pause the security system so it wouldn't go off when she entered.

Part of her wanted to tell him that she wished she had bulletproof bubble wrap for him, too, but she knew he would have to look for his father. She looked at him, their gazes locking.

"Be careful," they said to each other at the same time.

Grace held the eye contact a few seconds longer, needing it, and also needing the unspoken assurance they'd all make it out of this alive. Then, they bolted from the cruiser with her heading to the front door and him running to the barn to join the search for his father.

Obviously, one of the ranch hands standing guard inside the house had seen Grace coming and knew who she was, because he opened the door to let her in. She recognized him as well. Cooper O'Malley. Like her, he'd been born and raised here in Renegade Canyon, and she was certain that Dutton had vetted him as well.

"Jamie, her nanny, the cook and the housekeeper have moved from her bedroom and into her bathroom," Cooper said, motioning toward the stairs. "It's the second room on the right."

She nodded but didn't budge until Cooper had shut the door, locked it and reactivated the security system.

Grace could count on one hand how many times she'd been to the palatial house. Definitely a mansion, but the furnishings weren't what she'd call fancy. It was more classic cowboy, with its leather furniture and artwork of the prized horses and cattle that had been raised on the ranch over the years.

When she made it up the stairs and to the hall, she saw yet another hand, Taylor O'Malley, Cooper's brother, and he opened the bedroom door for her. No cowboy vibe here. It was the decor of a girl caught somewhere between childhood and teens, since there were at least a dozen stuffed animals on the pale pink bed along with posters of some K-pop singers.

"Jamie, it's me," Grace said, and almost immediately the en suite bathroom door opened. Jamie rushed out and into Grace's arms.

"Did you find Uncle Ike? Is he alright?" Jamie blurted.

Grace held her for a moment, silently curing the terror she could practically feel coming off the girl. "Not yet. Lots of people are looking, though, and we'll find him," she added as she led Jamie back into the bathroom, where there were no windows, thankfully.

The cook, Jeannie Ingram, the nanny, Millie Roberts, and one of the housekeepers, Ruby Bilbo, were near the tiled shower, and they all looked as frightened and concerned as Jamie.

"Tell me what happened," Grace said to the girl. Yes, Jamie had already spilled the basics to Dutton, but often people remembered small but important things when they repeated the account.

"Start from the beginning," Grace instructed. She kept her voice calm, hard to do, knowing the search was going on outside. Outside, where Dutton, her deputies, Ike and the hands could become targets.

Jamie nodded and drew in a long breath. "Uncle Ike and I came back here after we left the police station. He stayed in the truck, and I went inside to get my backpack."

"Was the delivery truck you saw earlier still here?" Grace asked when the girl paused.

"No. But a few of the hands were down by the corral. No one was near the house, though."

Well, someone likely was, but Jamie just hadn't seen them. Grace figured Ike's attacker could have been waiting by the side of the house, or even behind the perfectly manicured shrubs and hedges that threaded through the grounds.

"I went straight to my room once I was inside," Jamie went on. "And I didn't see or hear anyone. I got my backpack and then stopped to answer a text from my friend, who wanted to know when I'd be at school. Oh, and I went to the bathroom."

Grace tallied up the time, and all of that should have only taken about five minutes or so. Not much time, so Ike's abductor must have been close.

"And then what?" Grace prompted.

"When I went outside, the truck was still running, but Uncle Ike wasn't in it. So I looked around, thinking that maybe he'd gone down to the corral where I saw the ranch hands. But they weren't there, either. No one was." Jamie stopped, swallowed hard. "Then, I saw the blood on the seat. Did someone hurt Uncle Ike?"

Grace dodged that question. No way did she want to spell out the possibilities. So she went with a question. "Did you hear anything when you were looking around for Ike? Maybe footsteps? Or did you sense anyone moving nearby?"

Jamie shook her head, and the tears welled in her eyes. "Is this my fault?" she asked.

"No," Grace was quick to say. "Why would it be?"

"Well, if I hadn't forgotten my backpack, Uncle Ike and I wouldn't have been here." She went into Grace's arms again, and Grace held on to her, wishing she had the time to soothe her.

She didn't.

Grace eased Jamie back and met her gaze. "I need the four of you to stay here so I can go help look for Ike. As soon as we find him, I'll let you know. In the meantime, don't go anywhere near the windows."

"Because someone could shoot at us," Jamie muttered.

The girl's raw emotion felt like a fist squeezing Grace's heart, and she found herself brushing a kiss on Jamie's forehead before she hurried away. The sooner she got out there looking, the sooner they could maybe put an end to this. However, she'd barely made it back to the stairs when she heard someone shout something that she definitely hadn't wanted to hear.

"Fire!"

DUTTON HEARD THE shout from one of the ranch hands a split second after he smelled the smoke. It was coming from one of the storage buildings behind the barn, and Dutton ran as fast as he could in that direction. Ran but kept watch. Because this very well could be a ploy by the killer to lure him away from the house, farther from Grace.

Or it could be just a way of making him an easier target.

Still, Dutton had to go in. He had to make sure his father wasn't inside.

Dutton rounded the corner of the barn and saw the smoke billowing from the storage building, where they normally kept tractors, ATVs, a hay baler and other large equipment. There were no windows, but the smoke was coming out from around the large garage-style door.

Two of the hands reached the storage ahead of him and began trying to lift the door. Not easy, not with the smoke coming right at them, so Dutton drew in a deep breath and hurried to help. If the killer was going to strike, this would be a darn good time since it would take him precious seconds to draw his gun or to dive to the ground away from gunfire. He hoped the killer didn't just start shooting to try to take out as many of them as possible.

Dutton soon saw the reason the door wasn't budging. Someone had jammed a piece of wood on the side, and it was acting like a wedge to prevent it from opening. Blinking back the sting of the smoke in his eyes, Dutton yanked out the wedge, and the three of them lifted the door.

The smoke charged out at them.

He had to fight the coughing spell that overtook him, and despite his burning eyes, he fired glances around the building. It was one large area with no windows and no other exits. No working overhead lights, either, he realized, when he tried to turn them on. It was possible the fire had damaged them or else someone had tampered with them.

His gut told him it'd been the latter.

Hell. If so, then a lot of planning had gone into this. And

his father could end up dying in whatever sick game the killer was playing.

Dutton drew his gun and then covered his mouth and nose with the crook of his arm. And he stepped inside. He couldn't see any actual flames, only the thick white smoke, but he heard something. A thud, as if someone had kicked the wall, and he was pretty sure someone inside was coughing, too.

"Wait," someone called out to him.

Grace.

Dutton cursed again because he'd been hoping she was still inside the house. Apparently not. Here she was, right in the thick of things, and it's where she'd no doubt stay until the situation was resolved. One way or another. Dutton decided to try to put a faster end to it by hurrying into the cloud of smoke toward the sound he'd heard by the back wall.

As he got closer, he heard other sounds, too. Definitely coughing, and he doubted it was the killer. With all the planning, the killer would have likely been wearing a gas mask. And if the killer was, then he or she was almost certainly waiting for Dutton to be in a better position to kill him.

"Dutton," someone said. Not Grace this time. He was pretty sure it was his father.

That got him moving even faster, and then he realized someone was right behind him. Thankfully, it wasn't Grace. It was the two hands and Rory. The four of them continued to fight through the smoke to reach the back wall.

And that's when Dutton saw the figure on the ground.

There was blood on his head, and his hands and feet were tied. But he was moving and trying to speak, which meant he was alive. Dutton needed to make sure he stayed that way and that meant getting all of them out of there.

"Get him," Rory said. "I'll cover us."

Good thing, because the killer could be right there. Or on the way out to go after Grace. Dutton had to shove aside that thought and just do what was necessary. He scooped up his father, hoping he wasn't making his injuries even worse, and he started running toward the door.

His lungs felt ready to burst, and each step felt like an eternity, but he finally made it outside and into the fresh air. And he saw Grace. She, too, was coughing and trying to bat away the smoke while she kept watch around them, looking for any signs they were about to be attacked again.

Dutton didn't stop running. He moved his father away from the storage building and to the side of the nearby barn that was about ten yards away. It wasn't ideal cover, but it was better than being out in the open. And it had the bonus effect of getting Grace, Rory and the hands there, too.

"I'll call an ambulance," Rory said, taking out his phone. "And the fire department."

Yeah, the EMTs were definitely going to be needed. Ike's head was bleeding, and it looked as if someone had clubbed him. There were also marks on his neck that looked as if they'd been caused by a stun gun. Added to that, Grace had inhaled enough smoke that she needed to be checked as well. Hell, they all probably did.

"What happened?" Dutton asked his father while he untied him.

They were all still coughing, and Ike was shaking his head. That only caused the bleeding to get worse, so Dutton tried to stop him. Tried and failed.

"An ambulance will be here soon," Dutton said to try to soothe him.

His father's eyes were wild, pleading, and the headshaking continued. He tried to speak but couldn't get out any intelligible words.

"Not a fire," Ike finally managed to say, and even though the ropes were still on his hands, he tried to latch on to Dutton to pull him to the ground.

Obviously, Ike was trying to tell him about some kind of threat, but Dutton didn't know what. Until his father said one word that made it all clear.

"Bomb."

And just then, the storage building exploded.

Chapter Twelve

Grace sat on the examining table in the ER and waited for the nurse to finish stitching up the cut she'd gotten on her arm. A cut from a sliver of wood that had shot through the air when the building exploded. In the grand scheme of things, it was a very minor injury and could have been worse.

A whole lot worse.

If the blast had happened just seconds earlier, when Dutton, Ike, Rory and the hands had still been in the building, they likely would have been killed. She could have possibly been, too, since she'd been standing right by the door. It was somewhat of a miracle they'd all survived.

Of course, Dutton and she had been plenty worried about the effects the blast might have had on their baby so they'd skipped waiting for a second ambulance, and instead Dutton had driven her in the cruiser to the ER.

Thankfully, no one inside the house, including Jamie, had been hurt in any way and now the girl and the house staff were safely tucked away at the police station, where they were giving Livvy and Eden their statements about the incident.

Grace looked at Dutton, who was getting his own stitches on his forehead. He was in the chair next to her, not an ideal place for the nurse who was doing his stitching, but he'd refused to leave the room. She was actually thankful for that, but not because she wanted his protection. She didn't want him out of her sight.

Ike had been the one assaulted and put in that building with a bomb, but she was certain this had all been planned to draw Dutton, and probably her, too, inside so they could be blown to bits. That wasn't the MO the killer had used for the other two murders. However, he or she had maybe been willing to stray from the MO just to accomplish the task of killing them.

Her phone buzzed again, and she tried to read the text that Rory had just sent her. Hard to do that with the nurse right in her face. Still, she saw the message and relayed it to Dutton.

"Your father has two cracked ribs and a concussion. They're taking him down for more tests now."

Grace hoped those tests didn't reveal any more serious internal injuries, and while she was hoping, she added that maybe Ike would remember something that would help them figure out who was responsible for what happened. She hadn't been able to question him yet, and so far, all Ike had said was that his attacker had been wearing a ski mask. Grace figured that once he was thinking clearer, he might be able to recall some critical details.

Dutton's own phone dinged twice, and as Grace had done, he relayed the text to her. "All the hands have been treated and released. No one other than Ike required an ambulance. The other text is from Rory and a repeat of what he told you."

So Rory was keeping them in the loop. Good. Because at that moment it felt as if she and Dutton were trapped here in this ER room. First, she'd had an ultrasound, to confirm the baby was alright. Then, they'd both been examined to determine how much smoke they'd inhaled. Even a small amount was worrisome, since anything that affected her also affected the baby.

"Alright," the nurse working on her said. "Finished for now. Just wait here for the doctor to come back in and go over any test results."

More waiting, but Grace knew there was nothing she could do to hurry things along. Besides, she could still work while she was here. She could continue to get updates not only on the injuries, but also from the CSIs, who were now at the McClennan ranch, pouring over what was their new crime scene.

Grace sent off some texts to both Austin and San Antonio police departments to ask them about the statement from Brian's lover, Felicity, and the search of Brian's house. Both could be crucial reports since they could add to the circumstantial case against Brian.

Since that case wasn't anywhere near solid enough, she'd been forced to allow him to leave the police station after his lawyer had filed a complaint about being held for so long. She hadn't wanted anything like a legitimate complaint to allow Brian to wiggle out of any charges that might eventually be filed against him.

The nurse with Dutton finished his stitches, repeated a similar comment about staying put until they see the doctor, and she headed out of the room. Grace looked at Dutton then, at the fresh bandage on his forehead, and she felt the emotions flood through her. He was safe. The three of them were all safe.

For now.

Dutton stood and went to her, and he might have pulled her into his arms if there hadn't been a tap at the door.

"It's me," Rory said, and he opened it to peer inside at

them. No stitches for him, but he had several bruises on his jaw, where a board had smacked into him.

One look at his face, and Grace knew something was wrong. "What happened?" she asked at the exact moment she got a text. A text from the doctor who'd been attending the unconscious woman, Georgia Tate.

"Georgia died," Grace muttered, and Rory confirmed that with a weary nod. She finished reading the text from the doctor. "She didn't regain consciousness before she passed away."

Which meant she was taking to the grave any details she might have known about her killer.

"Three women," Dutton said, and then he groaned and cursed. He scrubbed his hand over his face and then cursed again when his fingers raked across the fresh bandage.

Even though Dutton hadn't known Georgia, she totally understood his reaction. It wasn't just the loss of life. Or the loss of potential critical information. It was the fact that the killer had murdered three women…and for what? For revenge? A warped vigilante justice to right old wrongs that could never be made right?

"You want me to notify Georgia's next of kin?" Rory asked. "Her sister went to her place to get some things, but she should be back here at the hospital any minute now, and I can tell her then."

Grace nodded. She didn't have the mental bandwidth to do that right now, and it had to be done before the woman's sister learned about it through some other means.

"Are you two alright?" Rory pressed, volleying glances at both of them. He added a third glance at her stomach.

"Right enough," Grace assured him, and Dutton echoed much the same. It was a lie. They were far from alright, but then everyone involved in this investigation could say the same thing.

Rory made a sound of agreement and then left, closing the door behind him. Dutton immediately moved toward her again, doing what he'd no doubt intended to do before his brother's arrival.

He drew her into his arms, being very careful not to touch her wounded arm.

This was a bad idea. Every part of Grace knew it, too. But that didn't stop her. She melted right into the embrace as if she belonged there. And felt the instant soothing comfort that only Dutton could provide. Even when she didn't want him to.

She braced herself for him to ask how she truly was, and she'd have to repeat the lie she'd just told Rory. Instead, he brushed a kiss on her forehead and then eased back to lock gazes with her.

"I saw something I shouldn't have," he said. That gave her a fresh jolt of alarm before he smiled and added, "On the ultrasound. The gender is no longer a secret."

Just like that, she relaxed. And smiled. "Since I've heard ultrasounds look very grainy, I'm guessing what you saw was a part of a body that's...obvious."

"Obvious," he confirmed. "We could just run with this newfound knowledge and start testing out names."

"Boy names," she muttered, knowing that would have been the *obvious*.

Again, this was wrong, but so much of it felt right, too. The baby was a boy, and Dutton was the one person who would understand this was one of the pregnancy moments. They were going to be the parents of a little boy.

"Mordecai," Dutton joked. "That's an old family name."

Grace shook her head, but she was still smiling. Yes, it

was good to think of something that didn't involve murder and attacks. Leave it to Dutton to come up with something that could ease this weight on her shoulders.

"Thank you," she whispered.

"You're welcome." He paused, keeping his gaze locked with hers. "You don't mind knowing the gender?"

She shook her head. "The timing is good. Like an unexpected gift. Though I would have been equally pleased had you seen nothing obvious and the baby was a girl."

"Yes," he quickly agreed. "Part of my dad fantasies involved old stereotypes of teddy-bear tea parties and me fending off boys who'd want to date her once she reached her teens."

It was odd to think of him having fantasies like that, but Grace didn't push for any other details of what his dreams for the future would include. In fact, it was probably time for her to move out of his arms and send off texts to try to get any updates.

She didn't do that, though.

Grace stayed put, and made things a whole lot worse by moving even closer. And closer. Until her mouth met his. It was just a touch, but it packed a punch alright. The heat didn't come in slow, gentle waves. This was more like a tsunami.

Dutton reacted. Of course, he did. He eased her even closer and deepened the kiss. In a flash, it turned into something much more. Hot and filled with need. Until it felt like foreplay.

Still, Grace stayed put, and she did her own share of deepening. Her own share of fantasizing, too, and this had nothing to do with tea parties and teenage dates. It was about this ache she'd had for Dutton for as long as she could remember. It was about the single time she'd made love with him. That's where her mind went. To the bed. To the sex. To those incredible moments when they'd forgotten about their pasts and given in to the need.

She slid her hand around the back of his neck, urging him to take more. He did. He took and moved his hand down to the small of her back, moving her forward until their centers met. Well, as much as they could with the baby bump. It was that reminder of the baby that finally forced Grace to come to here senses.

Gasping for air, she let go of him and stepped back. Way back. But even the space between them didn't cool the heat. It was right there, zinging between them, and willing her to go back into his arms. She might have done that, too, if there hadn't been another tap at the door.

Good. It was probably the doctor, who could give them the all clear to leave. They could go back to the police station, where they'd be surrounded by people and wouldn't be able to give in to the temptation of kissing again.

Or doing more than kissing.

Her body was all for that notion, but Grace forced aside those thoughts and called, "Come in," to the person who'd tapped on the door.

But it wasn't the doctor. Her mother took one step inside and then sort of froze, her attention sliding between them. Aileen's sigh told Grace that her mom had no doubt figured out what had just happened.

"I've interrupted you," Aileen said, and it wasn't an apology. "I came to see how badly you're hurt."

"Not bad. Just this." Grace motioned toward her arm and Dutton's forehead. "We were lucky," she added.

Aileen sighed again. "You were. You were damn lucky." She turned to Dutton. "I'm about to lecture the sheriff. I'd ask you to step outside while I do that, but considering you've got a killer breathing down your neck, that's probably not a smart idea. So you get to listen, too."

Grace stood there, more than a little stunned. Her mother wasn't prone to lectures, and in the time Grace had been sheriff, Aileen had never interfered in an investigation.

"You should be on desk duty, and you know it," Aileen said to her. "It's policy, and I know this because it's a policy I wrote."

"Policy isn't strictly mandatory," Grace said, but then she immediately waved off that comment rather than get into the interpretation of the department's guidelines with her mother.

The policy spelled out that officers should be put on desk duty unless there was a critical operational reason for them not to be. A triple murder investigation was the very definition of a critical operational reason, but the truth was, there were other cops who could have filled in for Grace in the field.

But Grace had opted against that.

"As soon as the killer is caught, I'll go on desk duty," Grace said. That'd been her plan all along.

Clearly, that wasn't enough for Aileen, though, and Grace knew Aileen wasn't a former sheriff at the moment. She was Grace's mother. And she was worried about her safety.

Aileen looked at Dutton. "I'm guessing you tried to talk her out of doing anything dangerous." She sighed. "Of course, you did. I might not like you, Dutton, but you're not an SOB. You're trying to keep the baby and her safe, and it's putting you at risk."

"I'm at risk no matter what I do or don't do," Dutton was quick to say. "The killer named both Grace and me in that threatening note."

It was a bad time for it, but Grace nearly smiled. Aileen had wanted to play the guilt card to get Grace to consider putting both Dutton and her "behind a desk" and out of reach of a killer. But backing off wasn't going to fix this. Not for Dutton and her. Maybe not for her mother, either.

"The killer didn't name you in the threat that was left at the last crime scene," Grace said to Aileen. "But if the killer is Brian, you know you could be the main target. Heck, you could be a target even if it's not him, since we aren't sure of the killer's motive. I'll ask you again to consider protective custody."

A muscle flickered in Aileen's jaw. "No protective custody. Because if I'm truly the endgame target, then I want to make myself available. Not so he or she can kill me," she added when both Grace and Dutton opened their mouths to object. "But because I believe I'll be able to stop it."

Grace groaned, and she went closer, meeting her mother eye-to-eye. "I don't want you in danger. But I understand that you are," she acknowledged before Aileen could object. "It's the same for Dutton and me. I want the killer caught, and that means we all need to take more precautions than we're comfortable taking."

"Like Dutton and you sharing the same air space," Aileen muttered.

Grace pulled back her shoulders, waiting for her mother to snap out a reminder of how much she disapproved of Dutton and his family. That didn't happen.

"Is the baby okay?" Aileen asked. "I figured you had some kind of tests and an ultrasound."

"Both," Grace verified, relaxing her stance just a little. She thought of what Dutton had seen on the ultrasound, though, and automatically placed her hand on her stomach. "It's a boy," she told her mother.

Aileen flexed her eyebrows. And then sighed. "A grand-son," she muttered, sounding almost happy about that. It didn't last because her gaze volleyed between them again. "I don't have to say that all this time you two are spend-ing together will fire up the gossips. Yes, I know gossip doesn't mean squat. Not usually. But in this case, it does." She fixed her attention on Dutton. "I've heard this baby has cost you plenty of business."

Grace turned to him, expecting him to deny it. But he didn't. "How much business?" she asked.

"Some," he admitted, but she suspected *some* was mini-mizing it and that her mother's *plenty* was more accurate.

Even though she hadn't huffed or done any of the curs-ing aloud, Dutton clearly picked up on what she was think-ing because he locked gazes with her. "I don't need local business to keep my finances solid. If locals don't buy the livestock, others will."

Grace would have questioned him more about that, but there was another blasted knock at the door.

"Probably the doctor," Dutton said and went to open it.

Again, it wasn't the doctor, but rather Wilson Finney, and the county sheriff gave Dutton and Grace a look simi-lar to the one Aileen had aimed at them moments earlier. Of course, now there was no lingering heat from the kiss in the room.

At least Grace hoped there wasn't, anyway.

Wilson shifted his attention to Aileen, and she, too, earned a cool glance from him. Probably because he blamed her for not doing more to get him elected sheriff. He probably thought Aileen had shown Grace some favoritism over the years, but if she had, Grace certainly hadn't been aware of it.

"I heard about what happened at the ranch," Wilson said, aiming his comment at Dutton. "Is your father alright?"

"He was injured, but he should be fine." Dutton didn't add more even when Wilson gave him a blank stare.

Wilson shifted to Grace. "I read the report you had Livvy send me about this Brian Waterson, aka Keith Cassaine."

Good. Grace had asked Livvy to send it to him in case he had anything to add to the original reports. Wilson hadn't been involved in the arrests, but he'd been a deputy then, and Grace had had Livvy contact all former deputies in case they recalled something that would help with the investigation.

"I have some vague memories of him and the teenage girl who died." Wilson went on. "And I heard him threaten Aileen. But I haven't had any contact with him in the past eleven years." He paused. "You didn't think I'd teamed up with him to kill those female cops, did you?"

There it was, that snark that had become Wilson's default reaction when it came to her, and as Dutton had done, Grace went with a blank-stare response. Yes, she had to consider that Wilson might have joined forces with Brian, but that was a long shot. She figured either the killer was working alone, or had hired a henchman to do some of the dirty work.

Like assaulting Ike and blowing up a storage building in an attempt to murder Dutton and her.

Wilson huffed. "I'm not a killer, and while you're obviously having trouble wrapping your head around that, I want you to know that I came here to help."

"Help?" she asked, and Grace wished she'd toned down a smidge of the shocked tone. "How?"

"By letting one of your deputies take a sample of the carpet from my cruiser and my personal vehicle," Wilson said. "That'll rule me out as a suspect."

It wouldn't. The only thing it would absolutely rule out

was that the fibers either did or didn't match the ones taken from the fence post. It definitely wouldn't prove Wilson's innocence. He still had means, motive and opportunity. It was his image on the sketch the police artist had done. And he could have been the one who'd orchestrated the attack at the ranch.

But Grace didn't spell out any of that.

However, her expression must have conveyed her suspicions about him because Wilson huffed again. "I had a second reason for coming here. I got a call from Cassie about a half hour ago, and she told me that the town council is meeting in the morning to discuss the recall process."

Grace managed to get her cop face on in time before Wilson could see the gut punch that'd given her. "Oh?" she said, trying to sound nonchalant.

Wilson attempted to hide a smile, but he obviously wanted her to see how pleased he was. "Yes. It's possible that by morning, a recall election will be approved and you'll finally be on your way to being ousted as sheriff."

Chapter Thirteen

Dutton hated the smug look Wilson was giving Grace. Hell, he hated pretty much everything about this jerk, whose pettiness over losing an election had caused him to launch this vendetta against Grace.

A vendetta that had caused Wilson to murder three women?

Maybe. There was plenty enough hatred for Wilson to do that and more. But Dutton recalled something. A little dig he could fire back at the jerk.

"I've heard you've got some serious opposition running against you in the upcoming county-sheriff election," Dutton commented. "And you're way down in the polls. I mean, it's not looking good."

As he'd hoped, that got Wilson turning his gloating face away from Grace and pinning his eyes on Dutton. "Serious opposition that I heard you funded."

Dutton shrugged. "I know Jacob Morales," he said, referring to the opposing candidate. "I've done business with him for years, and he's honest and not prone to pettiness and grudges." The remark hit home and caused Wilson's eyes to narrow. "I haven't kept my donations to his campaign a secret, but it's not common knowledge, either. How'd you find out about it?"

Of course, it wasn't just a simple question, and there was a whole lot of insinuation in it. Well, one big insinuation, anyway. That campaign contribution could be Wilson's motive for including Dutton in the death threat. Added to that, Wilson could have murdered his own deputy as a warped way of garnering some sympathy, which he might believe would help him in the election. Of course, if Wilson, Cassie and their cronies managed to oust Grace, then Wilson probably thought he could step into her job.

Dutton would do everything within his power to make sure that didn't happen.

It was bad enough that Grace was facing this moronic recall threat because he'd gotten her pregnant. Bad enough that she was having to deal with that while also trying to stay alive and find a killer. It would be just one more layer of nastiness if Wilson somehow managed to take her badge.

"FYI, I contributed to Morales's campaign, too," Aileen said. "And I plan to officially endorse him."

Dutton really enjoyed the flash of anger those words stirred in Wilson's expression. But his enjoyment was short-lived. Because it was way too easy to fire up Wilson's temper, but the man usually took that anger and aimed it at Grace. He didn't get a chance to do that this time, though, because his phone rang. So did Grace's.

Grace and Wilson took out their phones at the same time, and even though neither put the calls on speaker, Dutton could immediately tell that something was wrong.

"What? When?" Wilson demanded, and shock replaced the anger on his face.

"Read the note to me," Grace said to the person who'd called her, and she was experiencing plenty of shock, too.

Hell, had there been another murder?

"I'm on my way," Wilson blurted, and he headed for the door.

Grace stepped in front of him, blocking the door, and told the caller, "I'll get right back to you. Go ahead and text me a copy of the note and assemble a team. We also need to make sure no one is inside the church, so call the pastor and check that," she added before she ended the call and looked at Wilson. "Just stop and listen. You can't go charging out there."

Even though Dutton had no idea what was going on, he stepped in when Wilson tried to move Grace away from the door. He took hold of the man and hauled him back. But it wasn't easy. Wilson was strong, and he was hell-bent on getting out of there. Dutton was equally hell-bent on keeping him in place, at least until he learned what the heck was going on.

"I'm going to Bailey," Wilson shouted. "I have to save her."

"Then save her by thinking this through," Grace said, her voice level and calm, the exact opposite of Wilson's. She glanced at Dutton and her mother. "Officer Bailey Hannon has been kidnapped."

Dutton didn't have to ask who that was. Bailey was a cop in San Antonio. And she was also Wilson's fiancée.

Damn.

Did the killer have her? Was she dead? Was she the murderer's fourth victim?

He hadn't asked those questions aloud, but Grace obviously knew what he was thinking. "Kidnapped," she repeated. "This isn't like the murders. The killer didn't contact us for those, but for this one, he left a message taped to the front door of her house, where she was likely taken. Then, he or she made an anonymous call to SAPD so they could get the note and let us know what's going on."

"Kidnapped," Dutton muttered, and despite still struggling with Wilson, he forced himself to think this through. "What's the ransom demand?" Because there likely was one, and Dutton had a bad feeling he knew what it was.

Grace looked him straight in the eye. "The kidnapper has demands," she began just as her phone dinged with a text. She stopped, read it and lifted the screen to show Dutton and Wilson.

Wilson immediately stopped struggling. Good thing, too, because Dutton's main focus now was on that image. A copy of the note Grace had already mentioned.

"'Grace, here's what you need to do to save Officer Hannon,'" Dutton said, reading. "'Dutton and you get in a cruiser. I know you have one handy. And just the two of you come to the Hilltop Church. I've left the cop in the cemetery. Come alone. If you bring Hannon's boyfriend with you or anyone else, she dies.'"

So, a note from the killer.

"You can't go there," Dutton immediately told Grace. "It's a trap."

"I know," she confirmed on a sigh.

"You can't let her die," Wilson said. "You have to go. You have to save her."

No shout this time. It was barely a whisper, and it was filled with emotion. Well, it seemed to be, anyway. But at the back of Dutton's mind, he wondered if Wilson was putting on an act.

Because Wilson could have arranged this whole mess to kill Grace and him.

Yeah, that sounded extreme, to use his own fiancée, but everything about this situation was extreme. And potentially deadly.

"I told Rory to assemble a team," Grace said. "And he

will. You and I will go in a cruiser to the cemetery, and Rory
and at least two other deputies will be behind us. They'll
stay out of sight until we can figure out how the killer in-
tends to handle this."

"He'll handle it by killing Bailey if you two don't get
there now," Wilson insisted.

Grace shifted her attention to Wilson. "The killer will
have to communicate with us somehow. Maybe a phone
call or text. Maybe another note, since that seems to be the
preferred method. But unless he's an idiot, he won't expect
Dutton and me to speed up there and bolt from the cruiser
so we can be gunned down."

"I can go to the cemetery and park my truck on a trail,"
Aileen offered. "I can be backup to your backup."

Grace sighed. "And that could be exactly what the killer
wants. Remember, you could be the primary target."

Dutton could tell Aileen wanted to argue that. She was
a cop to the bone, and she wanted to help. She wanted to
try to protect her daughter and unborn grandchild. But Aileen didn't push. She gave a confirming nod.

"I'll go to the police station and wait there for news,"
Aileen conceded. "I'm guessing you'd rather me be there
than drive back to my place?"

"Yes," Grace quickly agreed, and she reached out and
gave her mother's hand a gentle squeeze. "Dutton and I
will be as careful as we can be." With that assurance, she
turned to Wilson. "And I want you to go to the station, too.
Use your own car," she added, but didn't spell out that she
didn't want him in the same vehicle with Aileen. "Don't
go near that cemetery, understand?"

Wilson nodded, but Dutton was nowhere near convinced
the man would stay put. Maybe because he was out of his

mind with worry over his fiancée. Or the man might go if he was the killer. Dutton just wished he knew which.

And that he could figure out how to stop this nightmare.

When Grace's phone rang, Dutton was close enough to see Rory's name on the screen, and she motioned for him to follow her. "Please make sure Wilson goes to the police station," she said to her mother, and Grace added a hard look at Wilson, no doubt to convince him to comply.

Grace and Dutton went out and into a hall that led to the ER itself, and she didn't answer the call until she was out of Wilson's earshot. She didn't put the call on speaker but held it close to both of them so Dutton would be able to hear.

"Made it back to the station about five minutes ago, and the team is assembled," Rory said, and he could hear the concern in his brother's voice. "Livvy and me in one vehicle. Judson and Eden in another. We're leaving now, so we should make it to the church ahead of you. What's the next step?" he asked. "And please don't say it's you and Dutton going to the cemetery."

"We're going," Grace confirmed. "But we're not getting out of the cruiser until I'm sure we aren't going to be gunned down. We'll try to get a visual of Bailey, evaluate the situation and wait for the killer to contact us. In the meantime, I want you and the rest of the team to park on the dirt road behind the church. Obviously, stay out of sight and look for any signs of trouble."

"There'll be trouble," Rory protested. "The cruisers are bullet-resistant, but Dutton and you can still be shot."

"We'll put on the Kevlar," she said. *"We,"* she emphasized. "Dutton won't refuse it this time."

He wouldn't. It was the smart thing to do in this situation, and Dutton also wanted to reduce any worry Grace had about him.

"Once the team is parked," Grace went on, "try to get into a position to cover Dutton and me if it becomes necessary."

"Of course," Rory muttered. His brother said something Dutton didn't catch. Profanity probably. "Just be careful."

"You and the team do the same," she said and then ended the call.

They started toward the exit where Grace had left the cruiser, but they didn't just bolt outside. After all, this could be the plan, to kill them as they were hurrying from the hospital. They stopped at the sliding glass doors and glanced around the parking lot. Dutton didn't see anything out of the ordinary, but that didn't mean someone wasn't out there, waiting.

Grace looked at him, but not with the harsh expression she'd aimed at Wilson. This look was loaded with worry. With regret, too. "I hate that you've been pulled into things like this. I wanted the badge. You never did."

"Never. I'm a cowboy to the core," he agreed. "But you might have been pulled into this because of me," he reminded her.

She certainly didn't latch on to that. "Either way, just swear to me you'll do everything humanly possible to stay safe."

"I will if you promise me the same thing," he countered.

Grace nodded, held his gaze a moment longer and then glanced around the parking lot again before she motioned for them to move. They did. Both of them drew their guns, hurrying to the cruiser, and they climbed inside as fast as they could.

Dutton had held his breath during the short dash to the vehicle, and he'd also braced himself for the sound of gunfire. But there was nothing. Apparently, the killer hadn't planned for the showdown here but at the cemetery.

She started the engine but then reached across the back seat to retrieve the Kevlar vests she'd left there. They put them on before Grace drove away.

"My mom is buried at that cemetery, and I've been there many times," Dutton told her as he kept watch of their surroundings. "There are plenty of places to hide."

"Yes," she muttered.

Like him, she had probably been there many times, too, and was probably trying to picture the place so she could calculate the best spot for the killer to lie in wait for them. The limestone exterior church was old, built over a hundred years ago, and wasn't huge by any standards.

The grounds were a different matter, though.

The cemetery spread out over at least three acres. Not a wide-open space, either. There were massive trees mixed in among the tombstones and yet more trees and shrubs encircling it. That's likely where the killer would be.

"Can you pull up a photo of Bailey on your phone?" Grace asked him. "There might be one on the SAPD website."

While still volleying glances around him, Dutton typed in the woman's name and almost immediately got a lot of hits. Since one of the top hits was an engagement announcement, he tapped on that one and saw a smiling Wilson with a tall willowy blonde who was sporting the same expression. It was strange to see Wilson like this, since the man was usually snarling, but the couple looked very much in love.

Looked.

Dutton hadn't ruled out the possibility that Wilson was a cold-blooded killer who might harm female cops to get back at Grace. However, would Wilson actually murder his fiancée? Maybe. But then there were a lot of maybes in this investigation.

He showed her the photo, and Grace made several quick glances at it, as if committing the image to memory. The hope was they'd find Bailey looking pretty much the same as she was here. Almost certainly not smiling, but perhaps she hadn't been harmed. Or worse.

Grace's phone rang, and he saw Livvy's name pop up on the dashboard screen. She took the call hands-free, and immediately the deputy's voice began to sound through the cruiser.

"The church is supposed to be empty," Livvy explained. "I called Reverend Michaels, and he said no one was scheduled to be there today, that he was working from home. They have a security system, and he insists it would have gotten an alert had anyone tried to get in."

Dutton knew security systems could be compromised, but he still doubted that's where the killer was. It was just far easier to hide in the woods. Added to that, if things went wrong for the killer, it'd be harder to escape from the church. Dutton was betting the SOB had a vehicle stashed nearby. A vehicle that hopefully the deputies would see and disable so the killer couldn't use it to make a getaway.

"We just pulled onto the dirt road," Livvy added. "Nothing out of the ordinary so far. What about you? What's your location?"

"Nearly there, about a half mile out," Grace answered and then paused. "I want Judson and Eden to stay in their cruiser so they can watch the road. Rory and you should put on Kevlar and ease your way through the woods, so you'll have a visual of the church. Watch every step, though. Remember, this guy's already used explosives and pepper spray. So far, he hasn't fired any shots, but that doesn't mean he won't this time."

Livvy made a sound of agreement, and they ended the call just as Grace took the turn onto the main road that led to the church. It didn't take long before the church itself came into view, since it was perched on a hill. Grace had to take the final turn before he saw the cemetery.

And he cursed.

Dutton had known there were a lot of graves here, but it suddenly seemed like hundreds and hundreds. And they weren't all low headstones, either. Some were actual mausoleums that would be the perfect place for launching an attack.

Grace slowed the cruiser as they approached the church, and both of them started combing the area, looking for both Bailey and the person who'd taken her. The driveway between the church and cemetery was gravel, and the rocks and dirt crunched under the tires of the cruiser. Not a deafening sound, but a distracting one that Dutton hoped wasn't drowning out other noises they should be hearing.

Such as Bailey calling for help. If she was alive, that is.

Or a killer moving toward them.

Hard not to react to that, but Dutton tried to keep his breathing and heartbeat level. He hoped Grace was able to do the same.

Grace continued the slow speed, inching the cruiser past the church, where they examined both the doors and the windows. Nothing was open, and nothing seemed out of place.

"He might have tied her to a tree," Grace muttered, a reminder that it wasn't just the church and cemetery they had to check, but also the woods.

Dutton looked there, too, while Grace stayed on the narrow, rough road that threaded between the headstones in the center and to the far back of the cemetery. Most people didn't use the road when they visited a departed loved one. They parked by the church and walked, but he suspected the road was for maintenance vehicles and gravediggers.

As the cruiser crept along, it meant a new area to search, and with each passing moment, the adrenaline just kept revving up. His body was obviously preparing for a fight that Dutton hoped didn't happen. He didn't want Grace and their baby in the middle of a gunfight.

He looked up and saw they were approaching the end of the road ahead. Once they reached it, Dutton suspected Grace would just turn around and keep driving through the cemetery until the killer made contact with them.

Or attacked.

The SOB sure wasn't going to make this easy, and Dutton was about to curse again when he saw something. A flutter of movement at the end of the road and on the right. Grace obviously saw it, too, because she hit the brakes and motioned toward the blond-haired woman.

Bailey.

Not tied to a tree but rather a tall column headstone. Her captor had used thick rope that coiled around her body twice and was no doubt tied in the back, where she couldn't reach it. Her hands were cuffed in front of her, probably with her own handcuffs, and for good measure, her feet were tied as well.

She was gagged but very much alive because she was struggling to get loose while she had her wild-eyed gaze fixed on the cruiser. That eased the knot just a little in Dutton's gut, but he knew the woman was far from being safe.

He had to fight his instincts to bolt from the cruiser and

rescue her. Which was no doubt what her captor hoped he'd do, with Grace in tow, so all of them could die.

Grace used the hands-free to send a text to Livvy. *We found her at the far back of the cemetery. She's alive.*

Maybe they would relay that to Wilson. Of course, if Wilson had orchestrated this, then he already knew.

"Why not put her in the middle of the graves, where it'd be harder for us to get to her?" Dutton muttered.

Grace made a sound of agreement. "Because this is both a trap and a way to torture all three of us," she answered almost idly and then made some quick glances over her shoulder. "Keep watch because I'm going to back up and try to get closer to Bailey. I'll have to run over some graves to do it, but I don't think the dead will object if it can save a life."

She threw the cruiser into Reverse, which caused some even more frantic movements from Bailey. Probably because she thought they were leaving. But Grace merely backed up a few yards and then drove forward, the right bumper of the cruiser scraping against a marble headstone while the tires crushed several artificial-flower arrangements.

"We're not getting out of the cruiser," Grace said while she got closer to Bailey. "What are the chances you can untie her and pull her through your window?"

"I'll make it work." He had to because there weren't a lot of options here. And it had to be done fast. Because he was certain that time wasn't on their side.

Dutton kept hold of his gun, kept watch around them, too, but he fumbled in his jeans and came up with a pocket-knife. The moment Grace was level with Bailey, she stopped the cruiser. So close that the passenger-side door was only a couple of inches from the woman.

He lowered the window and had to put his gun on the

dash. Grace would cover him, but it would still be possible for a gunman to shoot through the now-open window and hit both Grace and him. That's why Dutton worked as fast as he could.

Since Bailey was frantically trying to tell them something, he yanked down her gag and got to work cutting the ropes.

"The man who took me ran that way," Bailey blurted, tipping her head to the woods.

That gave Dutton a punch of hope. And dread. Maybe the deputies would be able to catch him and not get shot or killed in the process.

"Who took you?" Grace asked.

Sobbing, Bailey shook her head. "I didn't see his face. He wore a mask and used a stun gun on me."

That was similar to what had been done to the other victims, and Dutton was sure Grace would question Bailey about it further once they were away from this place.

Dutton continued to hack away at the ropes until he'd cut through them, and he immediately latched on to Bailey. This was likely going to give her some bruises, but it was better than dying.

Despite her hands and feet being restrained, Bailey helped by moving forward. Or rather staggering. She would have bashed her head against his had Dutton not caught her.

Grace didn't actually say "hurry," but he could practically hear the word repeating in her head. And he did hurry. Unfortunately, he also had to lean out of the window to be able to grip Bailey. Dutton steeled himself for gunshots.

But they didn't come.

He wanted to believe that was because the deputies had managed to apprehend the killer, but Dutton knew they weren't that lucky. In fact, that sense of dread went up a whole bunch of notches when he heard a sort of hissing sound.

Around them, the ground ignited into flames. Lots of them. They shot up hot and high in a circle around them.

Hell. The killer had set this up, and within seconds, the fire surrounded them. It wasn't actually touching the cruiser, but was so close that the heat felt like it was scalding him. The temperature was skyrocketing, and if they didn't move, they'd be burned to death.

Dutton gave Bailey a hard yank to get her all the way through and into his lap so he could close the window. The moment he did that, Grace gunned the engine, and the cruiser shot through the wall of fire and thick black smoke.

She couldn't see, of course, and that was a risk, but the biggest risk would be staying put and having the fire ignite the gas tank.

The tires kicked up the gravel, the rocks ramming against the undercarriage and the sides of the vehicle. And even though Bailey was blocking his view, Dutton saw the moment Grace managed to get them out of the fire. He had just a split second of relief.

Before the cruiser slammed into a tree.

Chapter Fourteen

Now that Grace was back in her office, she had given up on mentally complaining about having had to make yet another trip to the hospital. Because needing to go there for a checkup was a far better outcome than what could have happened.

Bailey, Dutton and she could have all been seriously hurt. Killed even, since they'd barely escaped that firetrap mere seconds before it could have gotten a whole lot worse. Yes, Grace had then crashed the cruiser because she hadn't been able to see what was right in front of her. But thankfully, the airbags had deployed, and none of them had been hurt other than a few nicks and bruises.

Still, it'd meant another visit to the hospital, and this time, Grace had looked at the ultrasound screen when the nurse had been moving the wand over her stomach. She'd seen her precious little boy kicking around inside her, and it had given her so much peace. The spent adrenaline had likely contributed to that peaceful feeling, as well as bone-weary fatigue doing its best to take over.

"As soon as you talk to Bailey, you should get some rest," Dutton told her. He was seated across from her in her office, and both of them were reading through reports from the CSIs and the deputies.

Or rather trying to do that.

Grace just couldn't focus and that's why she didn't argue with Dutton. He was right. She needed rest, and she wanted to be home. Only minutes earlier, she'd gotten a text from Judson, who'd let her know that her window had been repaired and her security system upgraded. And the work had been done by someone they trusted, the same handyman who'd been doing repairs for both her mother and the police station for decades. She hadn't wanted to take any chances with the killer or a hired gun getting into her house and waiting to attack them again.

The team of deputies that had been in the woods behind the church hadn't seen anyone running from the scene, but it was possible the killer or a hired gun had been there, watching, waiting for them to die.

Then again, he or she could have set the firetrap on a timer even before Bailey had been brought to the cemetery and tied to the headstone. It was something the CSIs were investigating, and hopefully, they'd soon have some answers.

Grace looked up when there was movement in the doorway, and because she was still on edge from the latest attempt to kill them, her body automatically braced. She had to stop herself from reaching for her weapon. Because this wasn't a threat.

It was Jamie, Ike and Rory.

Jamie immediately came into the room, and as Dutton stood, she threw herself into his arms. She wasn't crying, but it didn't look as if she could hold herself together much longer.

"I'd like to take Jamie and Dad home if that's okay," Rory said to Grace. "I can come back as soon as I drop them off."

"I've hired two bodyguards," Ike quickly explained. "And Dutton's canceled all deliveries and has posted one of the hands at the gate to make sure no one comes in. Another hand is monitoring the camera in case someone tries to sneak onto the ranch."

Grace nodded. Those were all good security measures, but she could add one more. "I can also arrange for a reserve deputy to stay with you."

Ike opened his mouth as if he might say something ugly about the offer. No doubt a knee-jerk reaction for him. But then he glanced at Jamie, and he must have seen the fear and weariness on the girl's face. Jamie had been through way too much. Ike, too. And the man must have realized that.

"Thanks," Ike muttered.

Grace muttered, "You're welcome," and texted Dispatch to send out a reserve deputy. She didn't have a lot of personnel who weren't already working the case. But there was a retired deputy, Mack Henderson, who would be able to fill in. Maybe, though, his services wouldn't be needed and the killer wouldn't go after Ike again.

Dutton held on to Jamie several more moments and brushed a kiss on the top of her head. "Text me when you make it home."

Jamie stepped back and looked up at him. "I will. And you'll stay safe?" she asked, glancing at both Dutton and Grace.

"We will," Dutton assured her. And they would indeed try to do that, but the killer was definitely hell-bent on killing them.

Well, maybe.

So far, the attacks had been life-threatening, but either they'd gotten lucky or else the attempts hadn't been designed to kill. They could be just ways of stringing out the torture. And that took Grace to the theory of Wilson being the killer. If the town was being terrorized, and made people believe she wasn't doing her job, then that would perhaps get the town council to vote for a recall election.

A recall that could cost her the badge.

The thought of that added a sickening dread to the rest of what she was feeling. All her life, she'd only wanted to be a cop, and now that might be taken from her.

Jamie said her goodbyes to Dutton and Grace, and the girl left with Rory and Ike. Grace started to turn back to the reports, but then Livvy tapped on the still open door.

"We might have something," Livvy said, and while she wasn't exactly smiling, she did look hopeful. "The church has two security cameras. Apparently, after some break-ins at other churches in the county, the pastor had them installed less than a month ago, so a lot of people don't even know they're there. Neither of the cameras face the cemetery," she quickly added. "But they cover both the front and back doors so they might have captured the attacker coming and going."

Grace felt some hope over that, too. "Please tell me the cameras save footage."

"They do," Livvy confirmed. "They're motion-activated so if a vehicle or anyone moved within their range, the cameras would have kicked in, and that would have been sent to the company that monitors it. We should be getting copies of that feed within the next hour or so."

"Good," Grace muttered. "When you get it, go through it, and if you need help, just let me know." She paused. "Are Wilson and Bailey still in the break room?" She hadn't seen them leave, but considering Wilson was a suspect, Grace hadn't wanted the man to try to sneak out with or without his fiancée.

"They are. I was just in there to get a cup of coffee, and they were on the sofa. Bailey said she'd come in here soon and give her statement. She just wanted a little more time to settle her nerves."

Grace totally understood that, but she wondered just how settled Bailey's nerves would be if she learned that her boyfriend was a murder suspect.

"One more thing," Livvy said, and this time, there was no silver-lining look in her expression. "Brian's lawyer is filing a harassment suit against you. I figure it won't go anywhere. We had more than enough to bring him in what with him lying to us and his boss about his alibi."

They had indeed had just cause. Still did. But Brian had likely wanted to do this in an attempt to make himself look innocent. It was too bad the SAPD cops hadn't found anything incriminating when they'd conducted a search of his house and the yard. According to the report Grace had been trying to read, everything the cops had seen meshed with the story Brian had given them.

"I'll let you know if I see anything on the church security cameras," Livvy said, and she turned to leave. She stopped, though, and sighed when she looked at Grace and Dutton. "You two are in some serious need of rest. Want me to shut the door so you can catch a catnap?"

It was tempting, but Grace shook her head, and on another sigh, Livvy walked away.

A closed door would likely mean she'd end up in Dutton's arms. And she might be the one to initiate it, too. Grace knew she'd find comfort there. But she'd find trouble as well. Because the barriers between the two of them no longer seemed to exist, and something as comforting as a hug could turn into a whole lot more.

"Security gate," Dutton said, holding up one finger.

"Ranch hand guarding the gate." A second finger went up. "Cameras that are being monitored." A third finger lifted. "And five other hands on the grounds who have licenses to carry and know how to use a firearm."

She didn't give him the flat look she would have doled out to him just twenty-four hours earlier. "My security system has been upgraded," she reminded him, but then Grace immediately waved that off.

An upgrade and the gossip it'd cause if she stayed with him—and it would generate lots and lots of gossip—was paltry compared to the security measures and backup that'd be available at Dutton's ranch. They'd both be safer there and so would their baby.

"FYI, if we're worried about us ending up in bed together, it could happen just as easily at my place as yours," he said. Except he didn't just say it. The words came out in that easy drawl that soothed and aroused.

Yes, even now he could remind her of the heat.

"Alright," she said. "We'll go to your ranch."

She didn't get a chance to see his reaction to that statement, though, because at that exact moment Wilson and Bailey walked in. And it was obvious from the slight smirk on Wilson's face that he'd heard what she had said. Despite the ordeal his fiancée had just gone through, Wilson seemed pleased that he might have more fodder he could use against her in a recall.

Bailey, however, wasn't smirking. Just the opposite. She was pale, and her eyes were red from crying. This ordeal had clearly shaken her to the core.

Dutton moved to the side so she could take the seat he'd been using, and the woman sank down onto it as if her legs were too weak to stand. Wilson dragged the other chair over to sit beside her.

"Have you caught the SOB who did this to Bailey?" Wilson snapped, aiming a hefty dose of anger at Grace.

"I'm working on it," Grace assured him and then turned all of her attention to his fiancée. "Bailey, for now, let's just chat in here. Later, you can make your formal statement. Is that okay?"

"Okay," Bailey muttered, and she practically folded herself into Wilson.

No way could Grace ask the man to leave or Bailey just might clam up, but Wilson couldn't be present during the formal statement process.

"I know this is hard," Grace continued, "but can you tell me what happened? Start with how you were taken."

Bailey gave a shaky nod and swallowed hard. "I was home, getting ready for work, and I heard something in my backyard. It sounded like a wounded cat or something, so I went out my kitchen door to check, and someone must have been waiting there. He immediately stunned me."

"He?" Grace pressed.

Another nod from Bailey. "Definitely a man, but he was wearing a ski mask so I didn't see his face."

Grace so wanted to ask if the man could possibly be Wilson, but she went in a different direction for now and hoped the woman was truly an observant cop. "Any sense of his height or weight?"

"I think he was about six feet, maybe slightly shorter, and had an average build. He was solid but not bulky and didn't have any trouble throwing me over his shoulder after he stunned me."

Bailey had answered that quickly, letting Grace know she'd given this some thought. Grace only hoped Wilson hadn't planted anything in the woman's head that would skew the guilt away from him.

Both Wilson and Brian were right at six feet tall, and both men had what she'd call average builds, so the description didn't rule them out. But Grace was betting this had been the work of a henchman. It would have been too risky for either Wilson or Brian to kidnap a cop in broad daylight.

"Anything about the man stand out?" Grace went on. "Did he say anything to you?"

Bailey shook her head. "He didn't speak, and he was wearing gloves so I couldn't see his hands. He was wearing black steel-toed boots, though." She stopped and shook her head. "I know that's not much. Lots of people wear boots like that. But there was nothing about him that told me who he was."

"Alright," Grace said, trying to keep her voice soothing despite the steely stare Wilson was giving her. "What happened after he used the stun gun and picked you up?"

This time, there was no quick answer. "I'm not sure," Bailey admitted. "Right after he had me, he jabbed me with a needle." She pointed to her arm, but Grace couldn't actually see the puncture mark because of the bruises and scrapes she'd gotten from being pulled through the window of the cruiser, and then the crash.

"The tox results aren't back yet," Wilson said, and even that was a snarl. "And don't you dare say I don't have the right to call the lab about that. Bailey's my fiancée. That gives me the right."

It didn't. Not legally. And especially since he was a suspect, but as long as Grace got the results, she couldn't see the harm in Wilson knowing them. Besides, if he'd been the one to arrange this attack, then he likely already knew what had been used to drug her.

"When I regained consciousness," Bailey went on a moment later, "I was tied to that tombstone, and I saw

Mr. McClennan and you driving up." She turned to Dutton then. "Thank you for getting me into the cruiser. You saved my life. You both did," she added to Grace.

"They wouldn't have had to save your life if she'd done her job in the first place and caught the killer," Wilson snapped, and it seemed as if he was geared up to do more lashing out, but Bailey gave his hand a gentle squeeze.

Grace was surprised that the gesture worked and Wilson seemed to throttle back a couple of notches.

"Why didn't he just stab me?" Bailey asked. She tried, and failed, to blink back tears. "That's the MO. Why did he let me live?"

"I'm not sure," Grace answered honestly. "This attack does break the pattern from the first two murders."

"But then there's the attack on his father," Wilson said, tipping his head to Dutton. "And the one at your house that left another woman dead. No pattern in those two."

"No," she replied. "But both of those attacks were likely meant to get to Dutton and me."

What she didn't voice was that the pepper spray could have been shot with a paintball gun that many people knew how to use, but using explosives and setting up a firetrap required some kind of expertise. Wilson might have that knowledge, but there were no indications that Cassie or Brian did. Then again, it might be something that could be learned from the internet.

"Pattern," Wilson grumbled. "That's the problem. You're looking for a pattern, and it's not there. That's because all this has to do with you. I think it's happening because the people of this town don't want you wearing that badge."

Grace lifted an eyebrow. "You think the killer is someone from Renegade Canyon? Someone who hates me? Someone who has a skill set that allows him or her to plan attacks like these?" She pinned her gaze to Wilson, letting him know that he fit that criteria to a *T.*

Wilson cursed, but before he could lash out, Bailey spoke. "Wilson told me you consider him a suspect because of the drawing the sketch artist did. The drawing based on what a little girl said."

"His cousin." Wilson jabbed his index finger at Dutton.

"Jamie," Dutton stated. "She's a good kid with an excellent memory and attention to detail. She wants to be a cop," he added.

That caused Bailey to smile just a little, but it was very short-lived, because Wilson went into anger overdrive.

"And the man she described just happened to look like me," Wilson growled at Dutton. "It reeks of a setup. If you get rid of me, then your girlfriend gets to keep her job. Well, I won't let you railroad me." He shifted his attention back to Grace. "This little chat is over. And you won't be the one interviewing her. Get one of the deputies to do that, but it'll have to wait. I'm calling a lawyer to sit in when Bailey gives her account of this nightmare you let happen to her."

With that, Wilson stood and practically hauled Bailey to her feet. Bailey's eyes widened in surprise, and for a moment Grace thought she might protest. She didn't. It seemed she had little fight left in her. Bailey allowed Wilson to lead her back in the direction of the break room.

Grace dragged in a long breath and got up to get a bottle of water from the fridge and take a moment to calm down. That didn't happen, though, because as Bailey and Wilson moved out of Grace's line of sight, someone else moved into it.

Cassie.

Great. Another round of what had been a hellish day.

Cassie was probably there to gloat about getting the town council to consider a recall vote.

"You have a minute?" Cassie asked.

Much to Grace's surprise, there wasn't any gloating or anger in her tone. Not even after Cassie got Grace's nod to enter and she stepped into the office, where she obviously spotted Dutton. Normally, Cassie's expression and mood turned sour when she saw them together, but apparently, the woman had something else on her mind.

"I heard about what happened at the church," Cassie said, easing the door shut behind her.

"I can't discuss the details of an investigation with you," Grace told her.

Cassie made a sound to indicate that's what she was expecting—that Grace wouldn't be sharing that kind of info. "Reverend Michaels said you were going to review the church's security cameras."

Grace didn't quite manage to suppress a groan, and wished the pastor hadn't revealed any information. Of course, it wasn't possible to keep something like that secret in a small town. Still, Grace didn't confirm that they would indeed be looking at the footage.

"I'll be on it," Cassie blurted. "On the security feed, I mean. I'll probably be on it."

That got Grace's attention, and she automatically adjusted her stance in case she had to draw her gun. From the corner of her eye, she saw Dutton do the same. Was Cassie here to confess to the murders? And was she about to launch into some last-ditch attack?

Grace prepared herself for just that.

Cassie would have had to go through the metal detector when she entered the building and likely wouldn't have been able to bring in a gun, but there were other weapons that could possibly be concealed.

"Why are you on the security feed?" Grace asked when the woman didn't continue.

Cassie huffed, but again, she didn't seem to be angry. "Because I was visiting my grandmother's grave. It's something I do on her birthday. Her birthday's not for another two weeks," she added quickly. "But I had some free time in my schedule so I went." She paused to draw breath. "I just wanted you to know in case you saw my car on the feed and, well, thought the worst."

Grace did think the worst, but then she was doing that about all of the suspects. This could be a clever move on Cassie's part—to dismiss why she was in the very location where an attack had occurred.

"When were you there?" Grace asked, though she would verify it once they had the footage.

Cassie checked her watch. "About four hours ago."

That could have been about the time the killer was setting up the firetrap and tying Bailey to a tombstone. But Bailey had said a man had taken her. One who was about six feet tall. Cassie was on the tall side, but she wasn't built like a man. It was possible, though, that Cassie had been there to assist someone she'd hired to help. Grace really needed to try to get a better timeline of events from Bailey once the woman was ready for a full interview.

"Did you see anyone or anything suspicious when you were at the cemetery?" Grace pressed.

"Of course not. With the murders going on, I would have reported it right away. It was just a routine visit to my grandmother's grave, and I had no idea about the cameras until the reverend mentioned them."

Grace considered all of that for a moment. If Cassie was

the killer, then there might be something on the footage that would indicate she had been there to help her henchman set up an attack. It was even possible the henchman had been with her in the vehicle.

"Alright," Grace said. "We should have the security footage soon, and I'll review it." And she wondered if it was just her imagination, but Cassie seemed very uncomfortable when Grace said that.

Cassie nodded and glanced at Dutton, who was scrolling through something on his phone. She opened her mouth as if she might say something else. Maybe about the town-council meeting that would be held tomorrow morning. But then, Cassie just muttered a terse goodbye and walked out.

Dutton reached over and eased the door shut. "Her grandmother's birthday is indeed in two weeks, but she has a lot of family buried there. In other words, Cassie could have used a variety of birth dates and anniversaries of deaths as an excuse to be at the cemetery."

Grace made a sound of agreement. "She could have had Bailey in the trunk of her car. Or maybe some of the equipment used to set up the firetrap." She stopped, considered that and wanted to curse. "There's no chance of me getting a search warrant for her car. It'd be seen as harassment for her part in pushing the recall. And, yes, I could just ask Cassie to allow a search, but the only way she'd agree to that is if she's got nothing to hide."

Dutton made his own sound of agreement just as his phone rang. "It's the PI," he told her as he put the call on speaker.

"Just got an interesting tip from a cop friend at SAPD," Jake immediately said. "Apparently, Elaine's parents realized a lot of money is missing from her savings account. About twenty grand."

"That'd be enough to hire someone to do some work," Dutton commented. "Did Brian have access to the account?"

"You bet he did," Jake confirmed. "My cop friend says they've got security footage of Brian making the withdrawal three weeks ago. They'll be sending the report over to the sheriff there once it's ready."

Good. It was yet more circumstantial evidence, but it was a legit reason to bring Brian back in to question him about it. Tomorrow morning, though, because Grace didn't think she had the bandwidth to conduct another interview with Brian until she'd gotten some rest. Of course, in the morning she might also have to deal with the fallout from any decision the town council made about the recall.

"There's more," the PI went on. "The camera footage doesn't stop there. The bank is near other businesses with cameras, and SAPD was able to follow the footage of Brian leaving the building. Once outside in the parking lot, Brian met with this man and handed him at least some of the money he'd just withdrawn. I'm texting you the picture of the guy he paid."

Within seconds, Dutton's phone dinged, and he cursed when he saw the image. Grace hurried over to him to see it for herself. The image was grainy, as most were from security cameras, but it was clear enough.

The man receiving the money looked like Wilson.

Chapter Fifteen

Despite trying not to think about it, one thought kept racing through Dutton's head. Grace was in his bed.

Or rather, she was in a bed in his house on the ranch.

He'd argued to get her here, and while Dutton still believed that was the right call, it wasn't easy. Because he wanted to be in that bed with her. Hell, he wanted to try to burn off some of this heat between them with sex. That wasn't going to happen, though, not tonight, anyway. Even if his body kept suggesting it.

Since Grace had left the guest room door open and Dutton had set up a makeshift office on the floor outside the room, he could hear her if she moved around. So far, she hadn't. She'd fallen asleep seemingly seconds after she'd muttered good night and gotten into bed. Dutton was thankful she was finally getting some much-needed rest, but he just couldn't seem to turn off his mind so he could do the same.

Not that he'd planned on a whole lot of sleep, anyway. No.

He wasn't just listening for Grace moving around, but was concerned about anything that could be a sign of trouble. The gate was shut, the security system was on and ranch hands were patrolling both the grounds and the perimeters of Dutton's place and the main house, where Jamie and Ike were. He had his laptop and was getting a continuous feed from the cameras by the fence.

Added to that, Ike had the two bodyguards inside with them, which was even more protection if the killer decided to go after Ike again. But Dutton thought the threat was over for his father. Not for Grace and him, though. He didn't believe the killer would stop until he or she got their primary targets—Grace and him.

Dutton intended to make sure that didn't happen.

He tried to get his mind off death and danger. Off Grace in his bed, too. And once again, he attempted to read the reports that Grace had shared with him. The SAPD one on Brian's withdrawal was thorough. The man had indeed taken money from his fiancée's savings, but there was nothing illegal about that, since Elaine had added his name to the account. Had Elaine been alive, she might have said she hadn't given Brian permission to take the cash. However, she was dead, so they only had Brian's side of the story.

Or rather, they would when Brian told it.

So far, the man was dodging another interview with his lawyer filing what seemed to Dutton to be delay tactics. Since Brian was a solid suspect, that strategy wouldn't last for long, though. Eventually, Grace would get him back into the police station to answer some hard questions. Like what had he used the money for. And who the man was that was with him in the parking lot.

The man who'd been the spitting image of Wilson.

Wilson's response to that was in another report. He'd insisted the person in the photo wasn't him. There'd been lots of cursing to go along with the denial and the accusation that Grace had a vendetta against him. Ironic, since someone had a deadly vendetta against her. Maybe Wilson. Maybe Brian or Cassie.

Of course, that led Dutton to another possibility, that the killer's crusade to kill them was because of him. And that led right back to Cassie. It was hard for him to imagine a woman he'd once had a relationship with now wanted him dead, but Cassie had seemingly been devastated when he'd ended things with her. But he'd done that after coming to the realization that he'd never love her.

Couldn't.

Because a part of him would always be in love with Grace. He'd felt that way about her since high school, and even though he'd thought the feelings would fade, they hadn't. They'd gotten stronger and hotter. Until they'd landed in bed five months ago. Now they were going to be parents.

Dutton wished though they could be a whole lot more.

But that might not be in the cards for them. If Grace lost her badge, it was possible she wouldn't be able to get past it, that a part of her would resent him for his part in making that happen. Dutton got that. He had plenty of resentment for the people who were trying to force her out of office. However, his feelings for Grace and their baby wouldn't change, whether or not she was a cop.

"Hell," he muttered under his breath. And he groaned. Why not just admit to himself that he was in love with Grace? Because that could lead to a Texas-size heart crushing, that's why.

He might have done some pity wallowing about that if he hadn't heard Grace moving in the bed. Dutton peered into the dark room and wanted to curse again. She wasn't just moving. She was awake and sitting up, and her gaze went straight to him.

"You said you'd sleep," she muttered.

"I will. I was just catching up on a few things."

She sighed and pushed her tousled hair from her face. "You're working, listening for any kind of break-in and keeping an eye on me. On the floor, no less."

Guilty on all counts, but he didn't want to explain that he hadn't been able to sleep because of thoughts of her. No, she didn't need to hear that.

Yawning, she got out of bed, causing him to groan. "You should try to go back to sleep."

"I will. Once the baby stops playing soccer with my kidneys." Grace headed to the en suite bathroom, but a few minutes later when she came out, she didn't go back to bed. She came toward him.

And Dutton felt his heart go into overdrive.

The rest of his body followed suit and began to rev up. Dutton hated to disappoint that part of him behind the zipper of his jeans, but he was still adamant that sex wasn't going to happen. He was still holding out hope that he could coax Grace back to bed so she could get more sleep.

"It's barely eleven o'clock," Dutton told her. "You've only been asleep three hours."

Grace nodded, retrieved her phone from the nightstand and continued to make her way toward him. There was nothing remotely sexy about the loose sleep pants and T-shirt she had on, but she managed to make everything look hot.

She sank down beside him, landing with her shoulder pressed against his, and she had a look at his laptop screen. "You're so much like a cop," she muttered as she read. "You keep this up, and you're going to lose some of that bad-boy shine."

"I haven't *shined* as a bad boy in a long time," he assured her.

"In this town, that never goes away," she said, and much of the lightness faded from her voice.

She was no doubt thinking of other things that remained in place, like the gossip about them. And the possibility of losing her badge. Of course, the thing that had to be weighing on her the most was the killer on the loose.

Dutton decided to try for some lightheartedness. "Yeah, gossips still mention the time I got drunk when I was a teenager, climbed on top of the roof at town hall and used red paint to scrawl pretty much every curse word I knew."

As he hoped, she did smile a little. "My mother took you into custody and made you clean up every syllable. You're lucky she didn't arrest you."

"I am," he concurred. "She probably wishes she had." He paused. "As for the other reasons for my bad-boy reputation, some events were greatly exaggerated."

"Only some. You went through that whole love-'em-and-leave-'em phase with many, many women. And then there are the business deals. All legal," she quickly added when he opened his mouth. "But some were cutthroat."

"Some," he admitted. "And others simply got enough attention to make me look ruthless. Like firing Wilson's father, for example." He paused again. "Or breaking Cassie's heart."

She looked at him. Not a good idea since they were sitting so close. It put her mouth much too close to his. Not good if he was truly going through with resisting her tonight.

"If the killer turns out to be one of them, this isn't your fault," she said. "It's theirs, and none of it is on you."

He wanted to believe her, but Dutton could still feel the

guilt. That must have shown on his face, too, because she leaned in and kissed her. Nothing hot and hungry. This was a kiss meant to heal. And it worked, but just a little.

Of course, it also worked to kick up that heat.

The heat that was always there. Always.

And that led him to do something stupid and he deepened the kiss. Despite the lecture he'd given himself earlier, he probably wouldn't have done more than just dive into the kiss. He would have pulled Grace into his arms and gone from there.

But her phone rang.

The sound shot through the hall and was so unexpected, Grace let out a soft gasp. "The phone," she muttered. "Not the security system."

No, not that, but Dutton instantly got a bad feeling when he saw Rory's name on the screen. Grace must have as well because she answered it on speaker and blurted, "Did something happen?"

Dutton knew she was steeling herself to hear there'd been another murder, but that wasn't what his brother said.

"Yes, something happened," Rory confirmed, and there was a helluva lot of gloom and doom in his voice. "It's your mother. She's missing."

Missing.

That wasn't a word any cop wanted to hear. Especially with everything else going on. Grace had to fight hard to tamp down the horrible thoughts that immediately flew through her head.

"Explain that," she choked out to Rory, though her throat had seemingly clamped shut.

She heard Rory take a deep breath. "About thirty minutes ago, your mother called Dispatch to ask for a deputy to come out to her place for backup. She said someone had just broken in."

Grace had to calm her own breathing, and beside her, Dutton cursed. And she knew why. It wasn't solely because of her mother's call and being missing. He no doubt knew the question Grace was about to ask.

"Why didn't she call me?" Grace demanded.

"You mother told Dispatch that you weren't to be contacted, that she wanted a deputy only." There was an apology in Rory's tone even though he'd had nothing to do with her mother's insistence. "I suspect that's because Aileen didn't want you to respond to her place this late at night, and she persuaded the dispatcher to do as she said."

Grace knew Rory was right, but her mother had been wrong to put Grace's safety over an active murder investigation. "Who did Dispatch send out to her house?"

"Bennie, but Ellie went with him," Rory explained, referring to Ellie Trainor, one of the night deputies who'd been on the job for nearly two decades. "I had already gone home, but after Bennie and Ellie arrived at your mother's house and found the door wide open, Bennie called me."

"And not me," Grace muttered. She was going to have a chat with her deputies and the dispatcher about following protocol for such things. Her mother, too.

If her mother was alive, that is.

Grace had to shut down any other possibility. Otherwise, she wouldn't be able to do her job. And right now, she had to focus on finding her mother.

She got up from the floor, and with Dutton right behind her, she went into the bedroom to change back into her work clothes. She didn't even care that she was undressing in front of him. Grace just wanted to be ready to get out the door as soon as she had all the details from Rory.

"Bennie and Ellie went into Aileen's house to search it," Rory went on. "When I arrived, they'd already figured out that someone had bashed through the back door and a window on the side of the house."

So possibly a two-pronged attack, maybe done at the same time to gain access and close in on her mother. It made her wonder which of their suspects and a henchman had done this. Or maybe they were both hired thugs.

"The security alarm didn't go off?" Grace asked as she yanked on her pants and then her boots.

"Not that we could tell," Rory answered. "There was a gun on the floor. A white-handled Smith and Wesson. And there were signs of a struggle."

The gun was likely her mother's since Grace knew she had one like that. What she couldn't understand was how the two attackers had gotten to Aileen without her being able to take at least one of them out. Her mother didn't have the physical strength to fight them off, but she had solid aim.

"Any blood?" Grace asked.

"None that I could see," Rory answered.

That was something to be thankful for. If the killer used the same MO, her mother could have been stabbed. Of course, it was possible the killer still had plans to do that.

"I called your mom's neighbors to ask if they saw anything," Rory went on, and that's when Grace realized he was driving. But where? Did that mean he had a lead, or was he coming to get her? "Mr. Henry said he saw headlights and that the car was moving fast. He didn't get the plates or a description of the vehicle, but he said it was heading south."

South would take them in the direction of the ranch.

Specifically to the pasture where the other two bodies had been dumped.

"Yeah," Rory said as if he'd read her mind. "Maybe returning to the scene of the crime, so to speak. I'm heading to the ranch now, and Bennie and Ellie are in their cruiser right behind me."

"We'll meet you," Grace said, and she knew that Dutton was about to protest and remind her that this could be a trap to lure her out. It most likely was. "She's my mother," Grace muttered, and that cooled the argument she saw in his eyes.

"Will you wear Kevlar and stay in the cruiser?" he asked as they hurried down the stairs.

"Yes to the first, and I'll try to do the second."

That was the best she could give him right now, and Dutton didn't push her. Probably because he knew she was frantic to find Aileen. Just as he had been when Ike had been taken.

They went to the garage, where Grace had left the cruiser, but before Dutton opened the garage door, he used his phone to access the cameras around the perimeter of the house.

"It's clear," he told her. "The two men you'll see are ranch hands."

Grace did indeed see the men the moment she backed the cruiser out of the garage. In fact, they weren't the only ones standing guard. She saw more scattered throughout the grounds all the way to the gate.

Dutton used his remote to open it, and Grace drove through, but she made herself wait until the gate was closed again before she sped away. She hadn't wanted the killer to be able to sneak in the moment they were out of sight.

There were no other vehicles on the private road, but like the cemetery, there were so many places for someone to hide and ambush them. Which could be the point of all of this. Her mother could be the lure just as Ike had been, and Grace hoped that meant Aileen hadn't been harmed, that she was being held as a bargaining tool or bait for Dutton and her.

Of course, Aileen would be furious about being used like that, and Grace knew her mother would do everything humanly possible to prevent Dutton and her from being attacked.

But humanly possible wasn't always enough.

Grace threaded the cruiser through the deep curves of the narrow road, wishing there'd been a full moon to give better illumination to the sides, where there were trees and trails. However, she did see different kind of lights ahead. The whirling blue lights of the cruisers. The two sets of responding deputies had obviously already made it to the fence.

Her chest tightened, and Grace realized she was holding her breath, waiting for the worst. A call to tell her that there was yet another body tied to the fence post. But none came, and that gave her hope. Hope that she had to clasp on to because she couldn't deal with the worst right now.

When they approached the fence, Grace pulled her cruiser behind the two others and tried to pick through the darkness to determine what was happening. All four deputies were out of their vehicles and had flashlights they were panning over the posts and the nearby trees.

Rory shook his head and started toward her. "Nothing," he said.

That gave her a jolt of sickening dread. She hadn't wanted to find her mother here, tied to a post and bleeding out. But if Aileen wasn't here, then where the heck was she? If this was a sick game meant to draw out Dutton and her, why hadn't the killer led them straight to him or her.

She lowered her window as Rory approached. "You got a look inside my mother's house," she said. "How much of a struggle had there been?"

The tightening of a jaw muscle let her know it'd been bad. But she hoped he wouldn't sugarcoat it. "Lots of things toppled over. Some broken glass." He paused. "It looks like someone shot into the wall. But no blood," he disclosed.

Both of them were well aware that sometimes blood wasn't in abundance if a cop-killer bullet was used. The Teflon coating on a bullet like that created all sorts of internal injuries, though.

"The killer's yet to shoot anyone," Dutton reminded her.

That didn't mean there hadn't been a gunfight this time. And if her mother had won that particular fight, she wouldn't be missing right now.

"Rory," Bennie called out. "You need to see this."

Grace's attention raced to Bennie, who was in a cluster of trees about fifteen yards from the fence. He had his flashlight aimed at something on the ground.

"What is it?" Grace asked as Rory hurried toward his fellow deputy.

Bennie shook his head, and it took Grace a moment to realize he wasn't doing that because he didn't know what he was looking at, but because it wasn't something he wanted to say. Finally, though, he spoke, and the words slammed into Grace like gunshots.

"We have a dead body."

DUTTON CURSED, and he automatically reached for Grace, who was in turn reaching to open the door of the cruiser. He figured she was in shock.

Which was no doubt what the killer had planned.

This way, Grace could be attacked when she bolted from

the cruiser, something Dutton couldn't let happen. He took hold of her arm and turned her to look at him. She struggled to get away, to run to her mother, and Dutton had to do something to stop her.

"Just wait a second," he insisted.

She did. With her breath gusting and panic in her eyes, she looked at him just as Bennie called out to them again.

"It's not Aileen," the deputy shouted.

The relief was instant in everyone at the scene but especially for Grace. The fight in her body drained away, and on a hoarse sob, she dropped her head onto his shoulder. Dutton felt her trembling when his arms closed around her.

Because she was no longer looking out the window, she didn't see the double takes Bennie and the other deputies seemed to have when Bennie inched a little closer to the body, fanning his flashlight over it.

"It's Wilson Finney," he said, causing Grace's head to whip up and snap back toward Bennie. "A gunshot wound to the head."

"Wilson?" Grace muttered, and Dutton knew her mind was whirling with the reasons for him to be murdered.

"No," Bennie amended a moment later. "He sure as hell looks a lot like Wilson, but it's not. Should I glove up and see if he's got an ID on him?"

Grace hesitated, probably because touching the body could destroy possible evidence. But there was a bigger picture here. The identity of this man might lead them to Aileen because Dutton wasn't buying that this guy wasn't connected to Aileen's abduction.

"Do that," Grace instructed. "Just be careful and make sure there aren't explosives or some kind of firetrap rigged around the body."

That put some alarm in all the deputies, and Rory went

to join them in using their flashlights to search the area. While they did that, Dutton eased his door open so he could be ready to assist Bennie, Ellie and Rory because this would be the perfect time for the killer to attack. Across from him, Grace did the same thing.

"I don't see anything," Rory relayed to her.

With that go-ahead, Bennie handed his flashlight to Ellie and put on a pair of latex gloves he took from his pocket. Dutton glanced at the deputy as he went closer to the body. His steps were slow and cautious, and like Dutton, Bennie and everyone else were volleying looks around the pasture and the trees.

It didn't take long for Bennie to ease a wallet from the dead guy's pants, and he opened it. Ellie turned the flashlight on what had to be a driver's license.

"His name is Teddy Lunsford," Bennie declared. "Thirty-one. His address is in San Antonio."

Grace yanked out her phone and did a search on the man. Dutton watched as Lunsford's photo popped up. Oh, yeah. He looked like Wilson. Maybe not an identical-twin kind of thing, but this guy could be Wilson's cousin.

"He's got a record," Grace added, and she cursed under her breath. "Eight years ago he was arrested for blowing up his ex-girlfriend's car and setting a fire ring around her house. She escaped, and there were no injuries, which explains why Lunsford only served six years in prison."

Well, that explained two of the attacks. Lunsford had likely done the one at the ranch and the cemetery. But there was something Dutton wasn't seeing in the report Grace had accessed.

"He doesn't have any obvious connection to our suspects," Dutton muttered. "Or to your mother."

Aileen hadn't been the one to arrest him. Cops in SAPD had. And Lunsford had served his time in prison hours from Renegade Canyon.

"No, nothing obvious," Grace agreed. "But there could be something."

She stopped, and he could feel the hope draining away. She had needed there to be something to help them find Aileen.

"Keep searching him," Grace told Bennie. "See if he has car keys because he could have a vehicle parked nearby. My mother could be in it."

That was possible, but it led Dutton to a whole bunch of questions. Would Aileen still be alive and had Lunsford been the one to take her? Also, why had Lunsford been killed? Was he a loose end that the killer had wanted to eliminate? If the last was true, then Aileen would likely be considered a loose end as well.

Bennie resumed his search of the body while Grace continued to go through Lunsford's background. Dutton was reading it as well, while throwing glances out the windows.

"Keys," Bennie called out. He held them up and pressed the keypad, no doubt to try to figure out if the vehicle was nearby.

It was.

The short beep sounded through the night. And it was close.

"I think it's on the trail just across the road," Dutton said, pointing in that direction.

Bennie double-tapped the keypad again and got the same beep from the same location Dutton had pointed out. Grace started the cruiser but then stopped. Dutton soon saw why when he spotted the movement in the rearview mirror.

A man.

He was behind the cruiser and coming straight toward them.

The adrenaline shot through Dutton, and getting off the seat, he stepped out and turned his gun in the direction of the man. Grace looked up from her phone, then tossing it aside, she got out also and took aim at him as well. The guy wasn't running, but he was hurrying.

And he had a gun.

"Everyone get down," Grace shouted.

That caused the man to stop in his tracks. "Is Aileen dead?" he called out.

Both Dutton and Grace cursed, saying nearly identical profanities, because they recognized the voice.

Wilson.

Dutton didn't ask himself why the county sheriff was here. He just kept his gun trained on him. Wilson had to know if he shot Grace that the deputies would open fire on him, but if the man was filled with enough hate and desperation, that might not matter.

"It's me, Wilson," he said after looking at the stances of the deputies, Grace and Dutton.

He had five guns trained on him.

Wilson did some cursing as well, and he shook his head in what seemed to be disgust. "You think I'm here to kill someone?" But he didn't wait for a response. "Well, I'm not."

"Then, holster your gun," Grace snapped. "And then you can tell me what you're doing here."

That amped up Wilson's disgust. However, he did put away his weapon. "Because I want to catch the person who nearly killed Bailey. I want to do your job for you since you're not doing it."

Grace ignored him and looked at Rory. It seemed to Dutton that she was debating with herself as to how to handle this. "We need to check out Lunsford's vehicle and deal with Wilson," she said, keeping her voice low, probably so that Wilson wouldn't be able to hear. "Dutton and I can take Lunsford's vehicle—"

"No," Rory and Dutton said in unison. Dutton held back and let his brother take over his particular argument.

"Ellie and I can go across the road in a cruiser," Rory insisted. "We'll be careful, and yes, we'll look for any traps. If your mother's there, we'll find her." He tipped his head to Wilson. "Bennie, Dutton and you can deal with him."

"Take Bennie with you," Grace told Rory. "All three of you should go."

Rory shook his head. "If Wilson's the killer, you'll need backup."

"Dutton is my backup." She glanced at him for a confirming nod.

But Dutton wasn't sure he wanted to give her a confirmation. He would have preferred Grace had an entire team of cops around her, but he understood it was important for her to find out if her mother was in that vehicle. Important, too, to get to her fast before she could be murdered like the other female cops.

So Dutton nodded.

"Go," Grace told Rory.

Rory groaned, but did as he was told, eventually. He hesitated a couple of seconds, probably hoping Grace would change her mind. When she didn't, he muttered some profanity under his breath, and he hurried to the other deputies to get them moving to the cruiser.

"What the hell is going on?" Wilson demanded. "They're

leaving?" he asked when Bennie, Rory and Ellie hurried to a cruiser. "Do they have a lead on the killer?"

Dutton huffed and was glad Grace ignored Wilson's questions and fired off some of her own. "Who told you about my mother, and how did you know to come to this spot on the ranch? While you're at it, you can explain why you're walking and not in your vehicle."

Wilson was slow to answer. "I have my police radio tuned to Renegade Canyon PD Dispatch. And before you say I don't have a right, I do. Bailey is going through hell and had to be sedated. Her folks are with her now, but they're a mess, too. All because you can't catch this killer."

"And you came here to catch him," Grace said with a whole lot of sarcasm in her voice.

The man shrugged. "Well, this was where he left the first two victims. So I parked up the road and walked here. I wanted to see what you were doing, and I figured my best shot at that was sneaking up on you and having a look for myself." He glanced at the fence. "Is Aileen here? Is she dead?"

Dutton shot Wilson a glare for the callous tone, and he so wished he could take the man down a notch. But now wasn't the time. Not when they were sitting ducks. Best for Grace to finish up what she needed to do, so they could go back inside the ranch gates.

"No, Aileen isn't here," Grace said, and her tone matched the icy feelings Dutton was having about Wilson. "Tell me about Teddy Lunsford," she demanded.

Wilson shook his head. "Who? I've never heard of him."

Dutton couldn't tell if the man was lying, but at this point, he was going to assume everything that came out of his mouth was meant to cover up his guilt in the murders and attacks. If Wilson turned out to be innocent, then Dutton would owe him an apology.

"Teddy Lunsford," Grace repeated, and she would have no doubt added more if they hadn't heard the revving of an engine.

A loud one.

Loud enough for Dutton to motion for Grace to get back in the cruiser. They did, both practically diving inside.

Dutton didn't spot any headlights, but there was definitely a vehicle coming from the road in front of them. There was a hill, and he didn't see the semitruck until it was coming right at them.

Chapter Sixteen

Grace couldn't throw the cruiser into reverse since Wilson was right behind it. Besides, she didn't have time to do anything before the crash came.

The huge black truck slammed into them.

It wasn't the kind of truck that was usually on the rural roads. This was a commercial vehicle that was double the size of the cruiser, and the driver was using it like a lethal weapon.

The impact jolted her back just as the airbag deployed and slammed into her face. It knocked the gun from her hand. Knocked the breath from her, too, and she immediately thought of her precious baby. Thought of what her OB doctor had told her as well, that an airbag wouldn't hurt an unborn child.

Still, the fear was there.

So was the fear of them being killed.

Grace started batting down the airbag, looking for Dutton. She had to make sure he was okay, and to check and see if the driver of the truck, or Wilson, was coming after them. She saw he was doing the same thing. He was frantically punching down the airbag so he could glance over to make sure she was alright. Then, he turned both his gaze and his gun in the direction of the truck.

"No cargo trailer, which makes it easy for the driver

to maneuver," Dutton muttered. "He'll try to come at us again."

Mercy. Dutton was probably right, and Grace tried to put the cruiser into gear so she could at least try to get out of the path of the truck before it immobilized them. If it hadn't already. The engine was on, but she wasn't sure if the vehicle was still capable of being driven.

She heard Wilson yelling, but she had no idea if he'd been hurt. Since he'd been standing behind the cruiser, it was possible he was hit. It was equally possible though that he was calling out some orders to his henchman, who was behind the wheel of that semi.

A henchman who could be hell-bent on trying to kill them.

The driver of the truck reversed, the massive tires sending up billows of smoke on the asphalt, and he sped back a few yards. Then, as Dutton had predicted, he came at them again. The first collision had taken out the cruiser headlights, and because of the height of the semi, Grace couldn't see the driver.

But she saw he was about to crash into them for a second time.

There'd be no airbag this time, but Grace was still wearing her seat belt. She prayed that was enough to keep her baby unharmed.

The semi rammed into them again, and the night was filled with the sound of metal crushing against metal. The front end of the cruiser crumpled, taking out the engine and mangling it as if it was an accordion. A part of the hood flew off, slamming into the windshield and cracking it.

Now they were trapped. And their attacker knew that. He continued the forward momentum of the truck, pushing them back.

And back.

The driver didn't reverse, didn't crash into them again. He just continued to push them backward. Grace stomped her foot on the brakes, hoping that would at least put up some resistance, but the brakes weren't working, either.

"He's trying to push us into a ditch," Dutton said. "And it's filled with water from the storms."

She glanced at her side mirror and realized that was exactly what the driver was trying to do. And once they were jammed into the ditch, killing them would be easy. Grace couldn't see Wilson and wondered if he'd be the shooter once they were trapped. If so, she didn't intend to make this easy for him.

Grace felt around on the seat and console for her gun, and for several heart-stopping moments, she couldn't find it. Finally, her fingers raked across it, and she snatched it up.

She glanced in the side mirror and saw the ditch was way too close. They'd be in it within seconds, and if the cruiser went in at the wrong angle and the ditch was deep enough, water could get inside and drown them. Added to that, they might not be able to get the doors open if the semi wedged them in.

"We have to move," Dutton said at the exact moment she was about to say the same thing. "Stay low, run to the back end of the cruiser and use it for cover. Keep a lookout for Wilson, too."

"You do the same," Grace insisted.

That was all they had time to say because the semi driver revved his engine again, and Grace knew it was now or never. She threw open her door, which thankfully hadn't been damaged, but her heart dropped when she saw that Dutton was struggling to get out.

She glanced at the truck, then at Dutton, and Grace

knew if she didn't do something, he'd be in the cruiser if the truck's tires managed to roll over the top of it. Or crushed it with Dutton inside.

Grace bolted out of the cruiser, then took aim at the truck's windshield.

And fired.

It was a risk since the bullet could ricochet off the metal. A risk, too, because she still didn't know where Wilson was, and at the moment she was an easy target, especially if he was still behind her. He could just shoot her in the back. But Grace refused to think about that right now. She only focused on getting Dutton out of the cruiser.

Dutton gave up on opening his door and scrambled across the driver's seat. Not easily. The now deflated airbags were in the way so he had to fight through those. And the driver just kept coming at them.

Grace took aim at the truck's windshield again, specifically targeting the driver's side of the vehicle, and this time she didn't fire just one shot. She aimed three in rapid succession. The bullets all slammed into the glass, shattering it. Maybe hitting the driver, too.

Because the truck finally stopped.

Dutton bolted out beside her, but he didn't stop. He took hold of her arm and got her moving away from the cruiser, away from the truck. And hopefully away from any bullets that the truck driver might send their way.

With each step, Grace steeled herself for gunfire.

But it didn't come.

There was only the menacing roar of the truck's engine and the sound of sirens. The deputies had no doubt heard the gunfire and were responding. She prayed that didn't end up costing her mother her life, but she had no idea if Aileen was even anywhere near here. The truck driver could be another hired thug doing the killer's bidding, and her mother and the killer could be anywhere.

They ducked behind some wild shrubs that weren't much cover but were better than nothing. Dutton immediately started shifting his gaze between the truck and their surroundings. Grace did the same. It was too dark for her to see the driver or anyone else who might be inside the truck, but she spotted a cluster of trees not far from a narrow portion of the ditch.

"There," she said, tipping her head in that direction. Moving there could get them farther away from the truck in case it came at them again. Plus, the trees would be better cover.

Dutton nodded and met her eyes for a split second. "Try to stay behind me," he muttered. "Think of it as desk duty."

Grace didn't especially want to take him up on the offer, but she didn't want to argue with him about this. She just wanted them both in a safer position so they could protect their child and maybe catch a killer in the process. The location by the trees might give them a better angle to see exactly who was in the truck.

Dutton sprang up from the shrubs, taking aim at the truck, and he started to move the moment Grace was in place behind him. She kept watch, ready for an attack. She didn't see anything, but she heard something just as they darted behind the trees.

Maybe a door opening?

Her gaze fired to the truck, but the passenger-side door was shut. She couldn't see the driver's side, though, and she was pretty sure Dutton couldn't, either.

They stooped there, with their breaths gusting, waiting for something, *anything*, that would help them pinpoint a killer. The seconds crawled by, the sounds of the siren getting closer. But even over the blare of that, Grace heard something else.

Running footsteps.

"I think someone just got out of the truck," Dutton whispered.

Grace agreed, though she still couldn't see anyone. Well, not by the truck, anyway, but she could definitely hear those running footsteps. Then, she caught a blur of motion from the corner of her eye and pivoted in that direction with her gun ready.

And then she saw something.

"Wilson," she muttered.

Dutton followed her gaze and no doubt also saw Wilson doing some running of his own. He was sprinting toward the tree line, where they'd found Teddy Lunsford's body. Was Wilson trying to retrieve some possible evidence that could be on the dead man? Or worse. Was there some kind of firetrap that Wilson was about to unleash?

"Wilson?" she called out.

He stopped and turned, and she thought he was trying to pick through the darkness to find her. "I have to go," Wilson said, tipping his head to deeper within the woods. "It's your mother. I just spotted Aileen."

DUTTON TOOK HOLD of Grace's arm when she started to bolt from the trees. He knew it was an automatic response for her, a desperate need to save her mother. But he couldn't let her run out into the open, where she could be gunned down.

Because Wilson could have just told a huge lie to make that happen.

They didn't know if Wilson was the killer, but the man was certainly on the short list of suspects, and if Wilson had indeed orchestrated this nightmare, then he likely wouldn't hesitate to use Aileen to get what he wanted.

But what the heck did he want?

That was a question that had kept going through Dutton's mind since the start of these attacks, but this all seemed extreme for someone jealous of Grace's badge. Still, people had killed for less than that, and maybe Wilson had as well. If so, that could mean he intended to use Aileen to draw out Grace and then murder both women.

Dutton wouldn't let that happen.

However, he also wasn't going to be able to keep Grace in place much longer. Both the cop and daughter in her were obviously urging her to do something and to do it now, now, now.

The deputies pulled to a stop near what was left of Grace's cruiser, and Rory, Bennie and Ellie barreled out. All of them had their guns ready. All fired glances around to try to figure out what was happening.

"Call for more backup and then check the truck," Grace told them. "But be careful. The killer could still be inside."

That was true, but Dutton figured those running footsteps they'd heard belonged to the killer. Maybe to Aileen, too, if the killer had forced her out of the truck and into the woods. Still, there was a chance that Aileen had managed to escape and was trying to put some distance between herself and the person who'd taken her.

Dutton watched while Bennie and Ellie kept watch and Rory went to the truck. And Dutton got a jolt of worry for his brother that Grace had almost certainly gotten for Aileen. But no gunshots came, and the truck didn't roar to life again to try to run them all down.

"It's empty," Rory said moments later. "But there's blood on the seat."

Grace made a sound, part gasp, part groan, and Dutton could feel the battle she was having with herself. Dutton wanted to remind her that Wilson had said he'd seen Aileen. Alive. But he had no way of knowing if that was the truth.

Not yet, anyway.

"You could stay here with two of the deputies," Dutton told Grace. "And the other deputy could go with me to look for Aileen."

She shook her head and stood, remaining hidden behind the tree. Grace motioned for the deputies to come to them. They kept the whirling blue lights of the cruiser on and made their way toward her. "We'll all go," she insisted.

Dutton had no way of knowing if that was the right call. After all, if she had stayed behind with a deputy, the killer might use that opportunity to sneak up on Grace and kill her. Or use Aileen to draw her out. At least this way, Grace would be with him, and he could do whatever it took to protect the baby and her.

"Wilson?" Grace called out once the deputies reached the trees.

No answer.

Dutton didn't hear any sounds of movement, either.

"How thick are these woods?" Grace asked him.

"Thick," he assured her. "But there are some trails and a few streams." Whether or not the killer knew about them was anyone's guess.

Grace nodded and motioned for them to get moving. They did, and Dutton figured there was no way for five people to stay quiet as they trudged through the trees and underbrush. The killer could be counting on that, too. He or she could be lying in wait for them.

The night air was heavy and damp. Almost smothering. It only added to the desperation and worry they were likely all feeling. Still, they kept moving and continued watching and listening.

Once they were away from the cruiser and were beneath the canopy of the thick trees, it became impossible to see, so Bennie turned on his flashlight to illuminate the way for them. The light would be another beacon for the killer, and if he or she wasn't on the run, then it would make them easy targets.

And it was indeed possible that the killer was running.

He thought of the blood Rory had seen in the truck. It could have belonged to the killer. Aileen was an experienced cop, after all, and she might have been able to injure the person who'd taken her. Maybe not a big enough injury to incapacitate, but it could give the five of them the upper hand.

While they moved, Dutton kept glancing behind them, checking for both Wilson and the killer. Who, of course, could be one and the same. But there was no sign of him. No sign of blood, either, as Bennie panned his flashlight on the ground in front of them. However, there were indentations in the ground to indicate that someone had recently gone this way.

They all came to a quick stop when a sound cracked through the woods. Not gunfire. Dutton thought this might be someone stepping on a tree branch. And it had sounded close.

Hell, was it the killer?

Was he or she getting into position to shoot them?

Dutton wanted to move in front of Grace, to try to protect her, but they were all jammed too close together for him to do that. Still, he tried to prepare himself in case he had to pull Grace to the ground.

"There," Rory whispered, and his brother pointed to a small clearing to their right.

Bennie immediately shifted the flashlight in that direction, and Dutton caught just a glimpse of the movement. A person wearing all black ducked out of sight and into some thick bushes and undergrowth.

And the person wasn't alone.

Dutton also spotted Aileen. Her hands were tied in front of her, and judging from the way she was walking, her feet were tied as well. She was gagged. Her captor latched on to her hair with a gloved hand and dragged Aileen out of sight.

Grace opened her mouth as if she might call out, but she reconsidered that, and snapped toward the deputies instead. "Rory, you, Bennie and Ellie try to sneak around on the right side. I didn't see a gun, but it's possible the killer is armed." She looked at Dutton. "You and I will take the left side."

To keep Grace as protected as possible, Dutton nearly argued for a deputy to be with them. But it was hard for a trio of people to sneak up on someone. Maybe the deputies would make enough noise to distract the killer, so that he and Grace could move in for the capture.

Or the kill.

Dutton wouldn't hesitate to end this SOB if it came down to it. He only hoped that the killer didn't manage to use Aileen as a human shield to try to draw out Grace. But that was likely the plan.

Maybe the truck had been damaged enough so it couldn't be used for an escape. That was the only reason Dutton could think of for taking this fight on foot. That, or maybe Aileen had managed to hurt her captor. That blood had come from someone, and he was hoping it was the killer.

Bennie turned off the flashlight, plunging them into darkness again, but that didn't stop them from moving. The deputies went to the right. Grace and Dutton, to the left.

Thankfully, after walking a few feet, Dutton's eyes began to adjust to the darkness, and he could at least make out where he was stepping. He couldn't hear anything, though, not over the pounding thud of his own heart.

His heart thundered even more when there was a slash of blue light that knifed through the trees. The cruiser. Maybe that was another distraction for the killer, too. Dutton just didn't want this snake focusing in on the deputies, Aileen or them so they'd be easier targets.

Dutton stopped when he reached the area where he was pretty sure there was a stream. Or at least there had been when he'd played here as a kid. And it was there, alright. The water coiled and snaked right in front of them. Not especially wide, but they had to jump to get to the other side. He prayed that this physical activity and stress wasn't taking a toll on the baby.

He and Grace landed together on the stream's bank, their boots sinking into the mud and soft dirt. They didn't stop. They just kept moving. Kept working their way past the trees and shrubs toward that clearing, where they'd last seen Aileen and her captor.

A sound stopped them. Not the snap of a tree branch but more like someone moving around on some twigs or dried leaves. They stood there, heads lifted, trying to pinpoint the direction. They both pointed to a massive oak at the same time.

Someone was there.

They didn't move directly toward the person. Staying low and walking as quietly as they could, they continued to go left so they could come up from behind.

Each step caused the knot in his stomach to tighten even more. Caused his fear about Grace and the baby to skyrocket. But they kept moving.

Until he saw something.

Aileen.

It was definitely her. She was wearing jeans and a shirt, and he'd been right about both her hands and feet being tied. She was standing by the tree right next to the person wearing all dark clothes and a half mask that covered the bottom portion of the face. The hooded jacket concealed the hair as well.

But not the knife.

Dutton saw it then.

The cruiser light caught the blade just right so there was a flash of a reflection. Enough for him to see that the person had it pressed right to Aileen's throat.

Was this Brian? Or Cassie?

Or some hired thug?

It was impossible to tell, what with the bulky outfit that reminded him of a grim-reaper costume. It could even be Wilson, if the man had managed to change when he'd run into the woods. It was possible he'd left clothes there just to pull this off. A disguise so he wouldn't be identified. Then, he could kill Grace and Dutton, maybe Aileen, too, and get away.

Dutton looked at Grace, and even in the darkness, they managed to connect gazes. She took a long, slow breath before she gave the nod for them to get moving again. They hadn't spelled out what the plan was here, but he was hoping Grace would let him tackle Aileen's captor. If Dutton got the chance to do that. He'd have to time it so Aileen wouldn't get her throat cut.

Their steps were even more cautious now, but Dutton knew they were still making some noise. Noise that the person in black must have heard because his head whipped up, and he dragged Aileen against him.

Dutton couldn't be sure, but he didn't think the person had actually pinpointed Grace and him. The killer seemed to be firing gazes all around, not just in their direction, but the side from where the deputies were no doubt approaching.

Grace stopped, reached down and picked up a rock. She hurled it toward the clearing. It got the captor's attention, and he whirled in that direction, causing the hood of his jacket to fall off his head.

Except it wasn't a *he*.

Dutton saw enough of the person's hair and forehead then. Enough to know who the killer was.

Cassie.

His heart dropped, and the sickening dread washed over him. Cassie was killing because of him. He was the reason that Grace, their baby and everyone else in Cassie's path were in danger.

And now he had to stop her.

Chapter Seventeen

Cassie spat out a string of profanities when the hood slipped off her head. She was wearing a stocking cap beneath it, but there was enough of her blond hair exposed that it was easy enough to tell who she was.

The killer.

Grace had no doubts about that now. Not with Cassie pressing the knife to Aileen's throat.

Cassie yanked Aileen even harder against her, but while she was glancing around, clearly spooked, she didn't seem to pinpoint Dutton and her. Maybe it was the deputies, though, since her attention seemed to be lingering in the direction they should be coming from.

"I don't see a gun," Dutton whispered.

"No," Grace agreed. "But she could have a hired thug nearby."

So very true. Lunsford was dead, but that didn't mean there weren't others. So this was either a standoff or a trap. Either way, people could be killed.

"Distract Cassie, and I'll sneak up behind her," Dutton muttered. "And please don't argue with me about this. I don't want you to end up having to tackle a killer with a knife."

Grace looked at him, and she mouthed a single curse word under her breath. Then, she nodded. "Don't you dare let her turn that knife on you," she whispered. "And save my mother," she added, brushing a quick kiss on his mouth.

Dutton didn't linger with the kiss, though Grace would have liked holding on to him for a moment or two. Even a couple of moments could end up being fatal for her mother.

"Keep watch for any hired guns," he said as his parting words, and Dutton began to make his way toward Cassie. He took more of those careful steps, obviously trying to stay quiet, but then Grace gave him some cover with her voice.

"Cassie," Grace called out.

Dutton wouldn't be able to see Cassie from his position, but she might be able to hear Dutton. The woman obviously heard her because Cassie pivoted in Grace's direction. Hopefully, Dutton was staying down and out of sight just in case Cassie did have a gun or there were any of her henchmen around.

"You want your mother alive?" Cassie immediately responded. "Then, you and Dutton have to trade yourselves for her."

"So you can kill us," Grace concluded.

"You both deserve to die," Cassie shouted. "Dutton loved me until you ruined things by getting pregnant. I could have worked things out with him. He would have come back to me, but no. You had to have him, and you played dirty by using that kid to make sure he was done with me."

And there it was. The motive was all spelled out and wrapped in the rage he could hear in her voice.

Cassie seemed to have a battle with herself to regain her composure. "All I need is the two of you and a vehicle to get the hell out here, and Aileen will live."

Grace doubted that. If it came down to it, Cassie would probably prefer to murder them all.

"You killed innocent people to get back at us," Grace

said. No rage in her tone. It was disgust, and she hoped Cassie's confession wasn't putting Dutton through a nightmare of a guilt trip.

"Innocent," Cassie growled. "Andrea Selby was a dirty cop. She deserved to die."

"Dirty?" Grace asked.

"Yes," Cassie insisted. "When I was putting out feelers for someone to help me set up the fires and such, Andrea volunteered to help. Well, volunteered if I paid her a hundred thousand. If not, she was going to rat me out. So instead, I killed her. I stabbed her and then tied her to the fence post on Dutton's beloved ranch."

Grace silently cursed. Apparently, Cassie thought Andrea's criminal behavior should be punished with a death sentence. But it was entirely possible that Andrea had just been trying to set up a sting operation to stop a killer from getting started.

"And what about Elaine Sneed?" Grace pressed. "Bailey Hannon and Georgia Tate? You can't convince me they were dirty cops, too."

"They were necessary kills," Cassie answered. "Or rather attempted kills since Bailey survived. But Elaine had to die so I could set up Brian. I needed someone to take the blame for this when I went on with my life. Without someone being convicted, your deputies would have kept digging. Loyalty," she said, spitting out the word as if it was a profanity. "Georgia because she happened to see me when I snatched Elaine."

"You left her alive?" Grace shook her head in disbelief.

"No. I intended to dump her at your place, but she fought me and got away. If she hadn't died in the hospital, I would have had to take care of her."

That caused the bile to rise in Grace's throat. This woman had no empathy for an innocent woman.

"And as for Bailey, I wanted to fire up Wilson to go after you for not preventing his fiancée's death," Cassie added.

"So, Wilson and Brian aren't part of your revenge plan?" Grace asked.

Cassie laughed. "I wouldn't trust either of those idiots. And enough of this twenty questions. You're stalling. Get out here now, or your mother dies where she stands."

"You know if you kill Dutton and Grace, then I'll move in to kill you?" Rory called out.

"And me," Ellie echoed, followed by Bennie's confirmation to let Cassie know all the deputies were nearby. "We'll also take care of any thugs you've hired."

"The thug is dead," Cassie muttered. "Lunsford was trying to blackmail me so I put an end to him. Self-preservation," she added. "It doesn't matter now, but when you cops dig, you'll find payment to Lunsford that looks as if it came from Brian."

So that explained why the man was dead. Explained, too, how Cassie had planned to get away with murder, literally, while incriminating someone else. Brian wasn't a stellar guy, but he didn't deserve to be railroaded for murder. He would have just become another casualty in Cassie's vendetta.

"Cassie, this is over," Grace ordered. "Put down the knife."

Cassie gave a hollow laugh that seemed to turn into a sob. "I know it's over," she muttered. No rage this time. Worse. Resignation.

Grace had a bad feeling that Cassie was ready to die. And take them out with her.

"Dutton?" Cassie shouted. "What do you have to say about this? This mess that you started when you used me and discarded me for Grace."

It hadn't been that way, and Grace knew that Dutton wouldn't even attempt to reason with the woman. He would just keep moving until he caught sight of Cassie. Once Grace saw him in position, then she'd have to do more than just stall by talking to Cassie. She'd need to move closer, to make it seem as if she was surrendering.

The sound stopped her.

Not Dutton.

It was nowhere near where he was walking. This was to her right.

Grace shifted position, watching, holding her breath, and a moment later, Wilson stepped into view. Unlike Cassie, he was armed, and he had his gun gripped in his hand. And Grace took aim at him.

"Cassie!" Wilson roared at the top of his lungs.

Oh, mercy. That caused the woman to turn, and Cassie put Aileen in a choke hold with her left arm and kept the knife at her throat with her right.

"Move away from Aileen or I'll shoot you where you stand," Wilson snarled.

Wilson certainly sounded enraged and ready to kill. And probably not because of any devotion to his former boss, Aileen, but because Cassie had nearly killed Wilson's fiancée.

"Come closer, and I'll kill her," Cassie said, sounding very panicked now, and Grace knew time was running out. "Grace, get me that vehicle, and you and Dutton show yourselves now. Now," she repeated in a shout.

With Cassie's attention now on Wilson, Grace welcomed the fresh shot of adrenaline she got when she bolted toward the woman. But Dutton came out of the woods, sprinting toward Cassie. Cassie heard the movement and turned.

Not fast enough, though.

Cassie was still moving when Dutton reached out and

caught hold of Cassie's right hand to get the knife away from Aileen's throat. Aileen helped with that. Even though she was tied up, she rammed her elbow into Cassie's gut and sent the woman staggering back.

Right into Dutton.

The body slam threw them off balance, and he and Cassie went crashing to the ground. Dutton kept a tight grip on her knife hand. And paid for it, since it gave Cassie the chance to punch and kick him. Howling like an animal, she sank her teeth into his arm.

Grace raced toward the fight even though she knew Dutton wouldn't want her anywhere near the knife. Dutton bashed Cassie's hand against the ground. Again and again. Until the knife finally went flying.

Losing her weapon seemed to break Cassie, and all the fight left her body. On a ragged sob, she went limp against him.

Dutton rolled Cassie off him, shoving her onto her stomach so she'd be easier to restrain. Then, he fired looks around, no doubt searching for Grace. She was there, alright, already in the clearing. So was Wilson. And the deputies were still a few yards away.

Wilson lifted his gun and took aim.

At Grace.

"Back off, Grace," Wilson snarled. "Cassie dies right now. I'm going to put a bullet right between her eyes."

Grace didn't feel much relief that she wasn't the man's target. That's because Wilson's eyes were wild, and he was clearly out of control. If Grace got in his way, he might shoot her.

"Don't do this, Wilson," Grace said. In contrast to Wilson's voice and expression, she was steady and calm.

"She has to pay. She nearly killed Bailey. And for what?

Because she couldn't handle a breakup with the town's bad boy?"

"Dutton crushed me," Cassie yelled, clearly regaining some of her fight. "He treated me like dirt. He's a monster, and he has to pay." She began to kick and tried to wriggle out of Dutton's grip.

Grace hurried to them to assist. So did the deputies. Since Rory and Bennie stayed back with Wilson, Ellie was the one who charged forward with her handcuffs ready.

"Back away from her," Wilson yelled. "Let Cassie get up so I can kill her face-to-face. I'm going to make her pay for the hell she put Bailey through."

Cassie let out another howl of outrage, and when Ellie leaned down to cuff her, Cassie ripped the gun from the deputy's hand. She bolted to her feet, the gun firmly in her hand. Grace's heart went to her knees as Dutton automatically moved to put himself in front of her.

Just as the shot blasted through the air.

The moment seemed to freeze. One moment, when the hellish thoughts flew through Grace's head and nearly brought her to her knees.

Because during that moment, she heard the gasp of pain and shock. She heard the voice and believed it was Dutton. And in that moment, she knew she couldn't lose him. It wasn't solely because he was her baby's father.

It was because she was in love with Dutton.

And he couldn't die.

She looked at Dutton, at the shock on his face, and she frantically combed her gaze over him, looking for blood. But there wasn't any.

Not on Dutton, anyway.

The blood was on Cassie, spatters of it on her face, and

despite the black clothes she was wearing, Grace saw the blood spreading across Cassie's chest.

The moment finally seemed to unfreeze, and there were suddenly sounds, a lot of them. People running, Rory shouting, and Cassie dropping to the ground.

Wilson was still standing, still holding his gun that had delivered the fatal shot, and he didn't resist when Bennie ran to him and yanked the weapon from his hands. Wilson seemed to be in shock, too. He just stood there, not a drop of color in his face. But he wasn't remorseful, either.

"Call an ambulance," Grace shouted, and she lowered herself to the ground, ready to attempt to staunch the bleeding or do CPR.

But it wasn't necessary.

Cassie locked gazes with Dutton, and she seemed on the verge of spewing more venom. That didn't happen, though. The only sound that came from Cassie's mouth was a death rattle as she expelled a breath.

The last breath she'd ever take.

Chapter Eighteen

Dutton sank down onto the foot of the guest bed and felt the bone-deep exhaustion wash over him. Understandable, since he and Grace had been up all night, tying up some of the ends of the investigation, and it was now nearly nine in the morning.

And the tying up wasn't over.

Maybe never would be. Soon, Grace would need to go back into her office and deal with the aftermath. Deal with any trauma her deputies and mother might have experienced, too. Along with speaking to the ME, who now had Cassie's body, and interviewing Wilson.

Yeah, there was plenty to do.

First, though, he was hoping Grace could get some much-needed sleep once she'd finished her shower. Maybe a really long one, so the hot water could loosen what had to be tense muscles.

His muscles were certainly tense to the point of being painful. But there was relief, too, and he was certain once he could settle his thoughts, he would realize just how damn lucky they'd gotten. Cassie was dead, and that meant her killing spree had come to an end.

Later, he'd have to deal with the guilt that his breakup with the woman had spurred the string of deadly events. But

Dutton wasn't so drained that he couldn't see that he wasn't to blame for Cassie's extreme reaction.

He just wished he'd seen it coming.

Wished he'd been able to stop her before she'd gotten started.

So, yes, he'd feel guilt over that and how close Cassie had come to killing Grace, their baby and him. Heck, Aileen, Bailey and so many others as well. Thankfully, though, Aileen was safe in her own home. Bailey, too.

Wilson, not so much.

The man had been arrested, and depending on what the DA said, he was facing some serious charges. It was possible that with a good lawyer, Wilson could argue diminished capacity, and he might just get away with that. Still, Wilson had killed Cassie, and Dutton figured the man's life would never be the same because of it.

The bathroom door opened, and Grace came out, bringing the scent of his soap with her. She was wearing a bathrobe, one that his mom had given him for Christmas years ago, and it swallowed her. Maybe it would be comfortable enough for her just to fall into bed and sleep.

He stood, ready to relinquish the guest bed so she could dive right in, but he stopped when she lifted her phone. Hell. Dutton hoped something hadn't gone wrong.

"Just got a text from Livvy," she said. "Brian will be cleared of any charges related to the murders. I can't charge him with being a cheating, lying slime," she added and then shrugged. "We'll have to let karma deal with him."

True, and Dutton was betting Elaine's parents would be firing the man. That was a small victory at least.

Dutton went to her and brushed a kiss on her cheek. He avoided any of the small nicks and bruises from the airbags and purposely kept it chaste, since he didn't want anything interfering with her getting some rest.

"Go to bed," he insisted.

He moved away from her, ready to head to his own bedroom and attempt to do the same, but she caught his arm.

"Stay in here with me," she muttered.

Dutton felt some other emotions cut through the fatigue. One was hope. Another was lust. And dread, since he didn't want lust playing into this, not when Grace had to be exhausted.

"Stay with me," she repeated when she saw the hesitation in his eyes.

The hesitation would have stayed firmly in place had she not kissed him. Her lips didn't land on his cheek, but rather on his mouth. And there was nothing, absolutely nothing, chaste about it. It was filled with heat and oh, so much need. More than enough need and heat that something inside Dutton snapped.

His resolve vanished.

And he forgot all about such things as fatigue and sleep. He only remembered this. The kiss. Being with Grace.

The memories came. Of other times they'd been together like this. Except this time was different. They'd survived going through hell and back, and they were alive. So was their baby, and that had Dutton stopping and taking a step back.

"You're pregnant." He hadn't intended to make it sound like some startling revelation, but his mind was definitely questioning whether or not this was a good idea.

Grace smiled, a rarity with everything that had been going on, and she pulled him back to her. "Pregnant women have sex. We're having sex," she confirmed.

His pulse was already revving, but that amped it up

even more, and this time when her mouth came to his, he was the one who deepened the kiss. He hauled her into his arms, and let the heat and need take over.

The kiss was instantly hungry, jumping right out of foreplay and into something with an edge. An edge that was demanding the sex happen now. Dutton was all for that, but he wanted Grace to take the lead in case there were some restrictions.

However, if restrictions existed, Grace was showing no signs of it. Kissing him as if he was the cure for, well, everything, she backed him toward the bed, then lightly pushed him back onto the bed. She didn't break the kiss when she landed on top of him, all without breaking the kiss.

She didn't waste any time going after his belt, and with her clever hands, she got it undone, all the while touching him and firing up the heat even more. Dutton decided to do some firing up of his own, and he yanked open the bathrobe.

And found a naked woman.

Fully naked. And despite the fire urging him on, he took a moment just to savor the sight of her. Her breasts. Her belly. And her center, where she straddled him.

"Perfect," he muttered.

She made a yeah-right sound that he would have almost certainly disputed, but she kissed him again, lowered his zipper and slid her hand into his boxers. That gave him a jolt and he went rock-hard. Instantly ready, too, so he had to do more reining in just so he could stretch out the pleasure.

Dutton pulled her down to his side and immediately leaned in so he could kiss her breasts. Her stomach, too. And then he went lower, lower, lower, his mouth trailing over her skin until he reached the prize. She moaned, throwing her head back against the mattress and lifting her hips.

Yeah, this was stretching out the pleasure, alright.

And he would have no doubt continued to stretch it until she climaxed, but Grace made a sound of protest and moved away from him. Not far. Just so she could remove his shirt. Then, she tackled his jeans, boots and boxers. She didn't stop until she had him fully undressed.

Grace took a moment, too, her gaze combing over his naked body, and she must have liked what she saw because she smiled. Their gazes met. Held. And in that moment, so many things passed between them. Things he wanted said aloud, but that would have to wait until they sated this need that was clawing away at them.

She had a cure for the need. And it was a surefire one. Grace pushed him back on the bed and followed on top of him. With the eye contact still in place, she took him inside her.

The sensations were instant. Hot. And almost overwhelming.

She paused a moment, to let them both settle, to allow her body to adjust. And then she began to move. Slowly at first. So slowly. Stretching out the moments until all he could feel was wave after wave of pleasure.

Just when Dutton thought he could take no more, Grace gave him more. By moving faster, taking him deeper into her body. Revving up everything. The heat. The need. And their bodies' demand for release. He held on, waiting until he felt her climax. Until he felt her muscles squeeze against the full length of his erection. Then, he waited some more. Held out as long as he could.

Before Dutton let Grace finish him off.

GRACE WAS HAVING an amazing dream. One where she was having the best sex of her life with Dutton. Then again, *best* was the key word when it came to making love with Dutton. That's why she was sliding into the dream, letting it play out while the heat consumed her.

But then, a sound woke her up.

Muttering a profanity under her breath, she slapped at the nightstand, the usual place for her phone. It was there, alright, but it wasn't her nightstand. That's when she remembered she was in the guest bed at Dutton's and that Dutton was still there.

Naked.

And she was snuggled in his arms.

No wonder she'd had the dream, and one look at his amazing face and body made her want to kiss him and go for another round of that great sex. But the phone didn't stop ringing, and it had woken him, too, so she reluctantly eased away from him and picked up her phone. Her heart got a jolt of a different kind when she saw her mother's name on the screen.

Since it hadn't been too long since Cassie had kidnapped Aileen and tried to kill them all, her mother could be dealing with the aftermath of that. Or maybe Cassie had had a henchman after all... Grace stopped with the worst-case possibilities and answered the call on speaker. Dutton would no doubt want to hear this conversation, since he could see her screen as well, and he was already sitting up. And judging from his expression, he was also bracing for the worst.

"What's wrong?" Grace immediately asked.

"I woke you," Aileen was equally quick to say. "I'm sorry. I probably should have let you sleep."

Grace checked the time and saw it was three in the afternoon. She'd been asleep for nearly five hours, and while her body felt as if it could use some more rest, that wasn't a high priority now. Her mother was.

"What's wrong?" Grace repeated, and she heard her mother gathering her breath.

"Nothing," Aileen insisted. "Are you with Dutton?"

Grace still wasn't convinced that nothing bad had happened, but her back went up a little at her mother's question. She hoped this wasn't about to turn into a lecture about her avoiding Dutton.

Because Grace wasn't going to do it.

No. No more avoidance. No more trying to convince herself she was better off without him. But that was something she'd deal with after she found out why her mother had called.

"Yes, I'm with Dutton," Grace said. "He's right here next to me and listening to this conversation." She left it at that, but her mother would know that meant she was in bed with Dutton, and since Aileen wasn't a fool, she'd know what had gone on.

"Good," Aileen replied, surprising Grace. "Because he'll want to hear this, too. The town council meeting just finished their vote about having a recall election."

Grace's chest went tight. She certainly hadn't forgotten about that, but she'd shoved it to the back of her mind. "And?" she pressed when her mother paused.

"And there'll be no recall vote. Grace, you got the endorsement of the entire town council. They think you're doing a solid job as sheriff."

That chest tightness vanished. "It probably helped that the killer is dead." And, yes, there was a tinge of sarcasm in her voice.

"It helped that members of the council realized they'd been letting a killer influence them about you. Added to that, the other person who spoke out against you, Wilson, is behind bars right now and will likely be charged with murder."

That helped with the remaining resentment that Grace felt over her badge being threatened. "Good," she muttered around the lump in her throat.

"I agree, and with Wilson and Cassie not spreading their hatred, I don't think any more questions will come up about you being at the reins," her mother concluded. "Oh, and I'm to tell you not to come into work tomorrow. That's from Rory. He's handling the postmortem on Cassie, and he and Livvy are doing the interview with Wilson."

Grace was mentally shaking her head. "I can't let them do that."

"Sure you can," her mother said. "Take tomorrow off. You've been doing nonstop duty to the badge. Now take a little time off for your baby. And for Dutton," she added. "Dutton, thank you."

"For what?" he asked.

"For keeping Grace and my grandbaby safe. I know that couldn't have been easy. It probably helps that you're in love with Grace. Yes, I can see that. I didn't want to see it for a long time, but I know you'll do what's right by both the baby and her."

With that, her mother abruptly ended the call, leaving Grace in shock. She figured Dutton was feeling the same, so she turned to him to give him an out. She would tell him her mother was wrong and that there was no need to do anything, no matter what her mother said.

She didn't get a chance to say any of that.

Because Dutton hauled her into his arms and kissed her. Really kissed her. It was long, deep and incredibly hot. The hotness went up a significant notch when he pressed his naked body against hers.

The remnants of the dream came rushing back. Remnants, too, of the scorching sex they'd had hours earlier. But

Grace got a jolt of other memories, too. Of Dutton being there for some of the worst, and best, moments of her life.

"I'm in love with you," she blurted when they broke for air. "And I want you in my life."

He froze, and for one horrible moment, she thought she'd blown it, that she had ruined this moment. But then he smiled. It was that cocky grin that could be considered foreplay. It certainly gave her another dose of heat.

"I've waited a long time to hear you say that," he drawled. "Because, Sheriff Grace Granger, I'm in love with you, too, and I also want both you and our baby in my life...oh, let's aim for forever."

Forever suited her just fine.

He kissed her again. This one robbed her of all of the breath she'd just gathered. But Grace didn't mind one bit. Because in that moment, that wonderful scalding moment, she, too, realized she'd also been waiting a long time to hear and say those words.

I'm in love with you.

They were absolutely true words. Ones that she felt with her entire heart, and she knew from the way Dutton kissed her, that it was the same for him.

So Grace pulled him against her, kissing him, and taking everything Dutton, and only Dutton, could give her.

* * * * *

Look for more books in New York Times *bestselling author Delores Fossen's Renegade Canyon miniseries, coming soon from Harlequin Intrigue!*